The Case of
the Safecracker's Secret

George sniffed. "Something smells funny."

"Maybe we've been locked in this vault too long," said Bess.

"Look!" cried George, pointing to the ceiling. Above them, a plume of gray smoke was wafting down from the air vent.

"Stay low," Nancy told them. Then she found herself choking. The unbearable smell seemed to fill her lungs. Beside her, Bess and George were gagging.

"What . . . is . . . it?" Bess asked weakly.

The awful truth came to Nancy through a sickly haze.

"It's poison gas," she whispered.

Nancy Drew
Mystery Stories

Available from MINSTREL Books

93

NANCY DREW®

THE CASE OF THE SAFECRACKER'S SECRET

CAROLYN KEENE

A MINSTREL® BOOK

PUBLISHED BY POCKET BOOKS

New York   London   Toronto   Sydney   Tokyo   Singapore

A MINSTREL PAPERBACK *ORIGINAL*

A Minstrel Book published by
POCKET BOOKS, a division of Simon & Schuster
1230 Avenue of the Americas, New York, NY 10020

ISBN: 0-671-66318-6

First Minstrel Books printing February 1990

10 9 8 7 6 5 4 3

Contents

1

An Inside Job

"So what does this bank guy want, anyway?" George Fayne asked Nancy Drew. "And why is he so desperate?" The two girls hurried up the steep main street of Bentley, Illinois, as George's cousin, Bess Marvin, trailed behind.

"Ooh, sailboats!" Bess cried, staring down the hill, over the small town's roofs and across Bentley Lake. The water glittered in the morning sun. Tiny white triangles crisscrossed each other as they glided along the silver surface.

"Hey, Bess," Nancy called over her shoulder. "We'd better pick up the pace or we'll be late to meet Alan Charles. Too bad I didn't park my car closer." Quickening her stride, Nancy sped up the hill, her reddish blond hair flying in the wind behind her. Her steady blue eyes burned with determination. She could smell a mystery in the air.

"To answer your question, George," Nancy said as they hurried, "I'm not exactly sure what Mr. Charles

1

wants. He wouldn't explain anything on the phone. All he told me is that he's president of the bank here and he needs our help."

"Interesting," George said, fixing her dark brown eyes on Nancy. She ran one hand through her short dark brown hair as she rushed to keep up with her friend. "And he found out about you because your dad used to be his lawyer?"

Nancy nodded. Her father, Carson Drew, was a well-known attorney in their hometown, River Heights.

"What really gets to me," Bess complained, "are these outfits we have to wear." She rolled her eyes as she took in Nancy's conservative light blue skirt suit, George's emerald green dress, and her own black skirt and white bow blouse. The girls had wanted to fit in with the bank's dress code in case they needed to do some undercover work. Bess usually liked to dress a little more flashily.

Nancy and George only half listened to Bess as they rounded the corner. Over the crest of the hill the Bentley Bank rose before them. Broad stone steps led through a row of white marble columns and up to two carved wooden doors.

"At last," Bess said, huffing and puffing, and finally catching up to her friends. "I knew I shouldn't have quit my aerobics class." Bess was just a little too fond of eating—she was always gaining and losing the same five pounds.

"We're late," Nancy said, hurrying up the bank's stairs. George, trim and athletic, bounded up the steps two at a time behind Nancy, while Bess lagged in the rear. Then Nancy pulled open the heavy door, and the girls stepped inside.

2

"Wow." George gave a low whistle that echoed in the cool, cavernous lobby. Her eyes opened wide as she stared up at the painted ceiling. Clouds and cherubs floated thirty feet above the girls' heads. A long mahogany counter with a thick Plexiglas window above it stretched the entire length of the room. Half a dozen male and female tellers stood behind it, helping a handful of customers.

"Pretty impressive," Nancy said.

A guard in a gray uniform walked over to the girls, his footsteps clicking against the smooth marble floor. "May I help you?" he asked.

"We're here to see Mr. Charles," Nancy told him. "We have an appointment."

The guard stepped over to the nearby security desk, spoke softly into an intercom, then nodded. "Past the tellers' windows, up the stairs, and all the way at the end of the hall," he told them.

The girls followed the guard's directions. At the top of the stairs a long, dark, windowless hallway spread out before them. Gone was the elegance of the main floor. The hallway went on and on, but finally, at the very end, they came to a door with a brass plaque that read, Office of the President.

"I'll bet he's about a hundred years old," Bess quipped.

Nancy knocked. A moment later the door opened, and the girls blinked at the bright fluorescent light that suddenly illuminated the dim hallway.

An attractive older woman with curly silver hair greeted them. "You must be Nancy Drew and company," she said. "I'm Elaine Kussack, Mr. Charles's personal secretary. Please come in. Mr. Charles is waiting for you."

3

Ms. Kussack wore tailored slacks and a blouse topped with heavy, old-fashioned costume jewelry. Somehow, Nancy liked her looks right away.

The woman led them through a small office with a desk, word processor, and coffee maker to another door, which stood ajar. Poking her head through the doorway, she called, "Mr. Charles?"

"Send them in, Elaine." A deep male voice answered her.

The girls followed Ms. Kussack through the door and into the inner office. Nancy heard Bess gasp as she got her first look at Alan Charles. Nancy felt almost as surprised herself. Instead of the aged banker they'd all expected, there sat a handsome man in his midthirties. His curly brown hair was just a bit tousled, and his blue eyes sparkled. His navy blue suit looked like the newest style from Italy. No doubt about it, Mr. Charles was quite attractive.

"Is there something wrong?" Mr. Charles asked, looking at Bess.

"It's nothing," Nancy said. She shot her friend a reproving glance, then explained, "Except that you look so young to be a bank president."

Mr. Charles smiled. "I just took over from my dad. He decided he'd had enough of banking, so he moved to Florida to play golf." He flashed them a winning smile and motioned for them to sit down.

Nancy introduced everyone.

"So, Mr. Charles," Nancy began as Ms. Kussack left, closing the door behind her. "You sounded pretty upset on the phone. How can we help you?"

The smile quickly faded from Alan Charles's face. "First of all," he told them, "you must promise that what I tell you won't go any further than these four walls. If word of this gets out to *anyone*, the bank could

4

be out of business in a week. My great-great-grandfather founded Bentley Bank. I can't let down four generations of my family."

"We'll keep your problem completely secret," Nancy guaranteed, and Bess and George nodded their agreement.

Mr. Charles heaved a deep, troubled sigh. "I hope you're as talented a detective as your father said, because something strange is going on here."

"A robbery?" Nancy inquired.

"Not exactly," Mr. Charles said. "Not yet, anyway. But a few days ago there was a mix-up in our vault."

"A mix-up?" Nancy asked. "What do you mean?"

Mr. Charles explained. "This past Monday a long-time customer of mine, Mrs. Unruh, came storming in here, telling me her two-carat diamond ring was missing from her safe-deposit box. In its place was a ruby and diamond necklace she'd never seen before. Then yesterday another customer, Mr. Abrams, reported that his wife's ruby and diamond necklace were missing—and that *he* had a diamond ring that wasn't his."

"Somebody switched them," Nancy said.

"Exactly," Mr. Charles stated with a nod. "As soon as I realized this, I called you. So far no one's pressed charges, because the property was retrieved—"

"But this means that *someone* has access to the safe-deposit boxes," Nancy finished for him. "Someone who shouldn't."

"Security's been breached," Mr. Charles confirmed. "And even if this person hasn't stolen anything yet, I figure it's just a matter of time. There must be at least a million dollars' worth of jewelry and valuables in our vault."

"The thing I can't understand," Nancy said, thinking out loud, "is why a thief would run the risk of

5

breaking into the vault and then not take anything. Think of all the work to get inside, and all that was accomplished was an accidental switching of some jewels."

"I can't explain it," Mr. Charles said. "But I do know that once there *is* a robbery, or if our customers hear about what happened, there's going to be panic. People will be pulling their money out of here so fast that—"

"Excuse me, Mr. Charles."

Nancy turned, startled at the sound of Ms. Kussack's voice. She'd been so intent on what Alan Charles had been saying that she hadn't heard her enter the room.

"I'm sorry to interrupt," Ms. Kussack went on, "but I thought you all might like some coffee or hot chocolate."

"None for me, thanks," Mr. Charles replied. The girls shook their heads no.

"You don't know what you're missing," the secretary said. "This is real Swiss chocolate. Once you try it, you'll never drink any other kind."

Mr. Charles smiled as Ms. Kussack ducked out of the room. "It really *is* good hot chocolate," he told the girls, "but she sounds like a commercial sometimes."

The smile disappeared as Mr. Charles got back to business. "This safe-deposit box switch has to be an inside job," he said. "Only a few bank employees have access to the vault. And our security system would be virtually impossible for an outsider to crack."

"How do safe-deposit boxes work?" Bess asked.

"It's pretty simple," Mr. Charles explained. "Each box requires two keys. The customer has one, and we have the other."

"So for a bank employee to break into a box, he or she would need a copy of the customer's key as well as

6

the bank's key," Nancy concluded. "Do you keep duplicates of the customers' keys?"

"Yes," Mr. Charles said. "I have them securely locked in my private safe. And I'm the only one who knows the combination."

"Are they in there now?" Nancy asked.

"That's the problem," Mr. Charles answered. "When I checked after the mix-up, the keys were gone!" He stood up and paced up and down in front of the girls, clearly upset. "I have to get this straightened out right away or it will be a catastrophe for the bank."

"This *is* a mystery," Nancy said. Pulling a small notepad and pen out of her purse, she made a few notes about what Mr. Charles had told her. "We'd better get started at once. Where exactly is the vault located?"

"In the basement," Mr. Charles told her. "I'll take you down there after we're through."

Nancy made another note on her pad. "What about video security?" she asked. "I noticed a camera in the lobby. Is there one in the vault?"

Mr. Charles nodded. "We keep the camera recording all night and review the videotape each morning. But in this case the videotape was erased! I still don't know how they managed to open up the camera. Its casing is made of solid steel."

"What about the camera on the main floor?" Nancy asked.

"The tape was there," Mr. Charles said, "and it hadn't been erased. But there was no record of anyone entering or leaving the building. And the night watchman didn't hear or see anything unusual."

"Maybe the watchman did it," Bess suggested.

"That would be pretty unlikely," Mr. Charles said. "He doesn't know any of the codes to open the vault, and there's no way anyone could get in without them."

7

"Do you have any suspects?" Nancy asked. "Any ideas at all about who it might be?"

Mr. Charles's worried gaze met Nancy's intent blue eyes, and she saw his expression begin to crumble. "No," he replied miserably. "I've always trusted my employees. I was sure they were completely trustworthy. And now I find out that—that they're not."

Nancy couldn't help but feel sorry for the bank president. "Well, maybe just one of them isn't," she said, trying to console him. Then she turned to Bess and George. "It looks like we've got our work cut out for us," she said.

"Then you think you can solve this case?" Mr. Charles asked, glancing hopefully toward Nancy. "It sounds impossible."

"Nothing's impossible for Nancy," Bess replied proudly.

"Before we start our investigation, we have a few details to work out," Nancy said, ignoring the compliment. "If we're going to hang around the bank for a while, we'll need some sort of cover."

"I've already thought of that," Mr. Charles told them with a smile. "I'll give you all jobs at the bank."

"Won't that look suspicious?" George asked. "Three new employees—especially such young ones—at the same time?"

"Not at all," Mr. Charles said. "Many of our tellers are college students who work only part time. Bess and George, I'll put you in our on-the-job training program. That's run by our head teller, Maurice Grun. Nancy, since you'll probably need more flexibility, I'll just call you an intern. That way you can wander around and ask as many questions as you like."

"Sounds good," Nancy agreed. "Well, I guess we're ready to start our 'jobs.' The first thing I'd like to see is

8

the vault, but it will look too suspicious if all three of us go. Maybe Bess and George could start their training with Maurice Grun while you and I go down to the basement." Nancy tucked her notepad back into her purse, and the group followed Mr. Charles out of the office. They nodded to Ms. Kussack as they hurried past her desk, then walked out into the dim, endless hallway and down the stairs.

But as they arrived for the second time that day in the lobby, it was no longer the hushed, calm place they'd seen before. A crowd of customers gathered around one of the tellers' windows. Nancy couldn't see what they were looking at, but she heard crashing noises and the sounds of heavy metal objects being thrown to the floor. Then a woman's voice pierced the hubbub, echoing across the lobby.

"I hate you!" the woman screamed. "I'll hate you till the day I die!"

2

Ransacked!

Mr. Charles pushed his way through the crowd toward the scream. Nancy motioned for George and Bess to stay back. If all three of them moved together, they'd blow their cover as strangers who'd just happened to get jobs in the bank at the same time. She squeezed between the people, trailing after Mr. Charles.

Peering through the Plexiglas that separated the lobby from the tellers' area, she could see a few of the tellers holding a man and a woman apart. Metal boxes and money were scattered all over the floor.

"You're a rat, Maurice Grun! A two-timing, two-faced rat!" the woman screamed. She struggled to break free from the arms that restrained her. Though the woman's voice was incredibly loud, she herself was petite. Nancy's gaze took in the slim, attractively dressed young woman with the fire in her eyes. The man she spat her words at was also young, but balding, and there was a sheepish expression on his face.

"Come with me, Nancy," Mr. Charles instructed as

he hurried through a side door leading into the tellers' area. "What's going on?" he boomed, taking control of the situation.

The tellers sprang apart at the appearance of the bank president, while the furious woman and the sheepish man glanced at him uncomfortably.

The man stepped over the mess of boxes and money, nervously biting his lip. "I'm sorry about the disturbance, Mr. Charles," he muttered softly.

"Would you like to explain yourself, Maurice?" Mr. Charles asked, looking almost as angry as the woman had a moment before.

"I'd rather not," Maurice said. "I mean, I don't think I should. It's a personal matter."

"Jill?" Mr. Charles asked sharply, turning upon the young woman.

By now there were tears streaming down her face. She could barely speak, so she just shook her head no.

Mr. Charles stared from one to the other for one more furious moment. "Okay," he said, frowning. "I can't force you to explain. But I'm warning you—your behavior is extremely unprofessional. If you both weren't excellent employees ordinarily, I'd fire you immediately for this. And if you can't control yourselves from now on, you'd better start looking for new jobs."

Suddenly the fire was back in Jill's eyes. "That's the best idea I've heard all day," she said passionately. "I quit!" So saying, she dashed over to one of the teller windows and snatched her purse out of a drawer. Flipping her hair angrily over one shoulder, she stormed out of the tellers' area and out the bank's huge double doors. As the sound of the slamming doors echoed through the bank lobby, everyone just stared at one another, looking a bit stunned.

11

Nancy was the first to recover, but she knew she couldn't say anything or she'd blow her cover as a new intern. In a moment Mr. Charles took charge. "Ladies and gentlemen," he addressed the customers through the Plexiglas, "I'm very sorry about this disturbance. Our staff will be able to assist you shortly." Turning to the tellers, he instructed, "Back to work, everybody. Maurice, I want you to pick up those cash boxes and make sure every dollar is accounted for."

"Yes, sir," Maurice replied, looking embarrassed but glad to have held on to his job. Obediently, he stooped to pick up a box, then began scooping money into it.

As his fingers flew through the bills, Nancy studied the head teller closely. He was such a nervous person. Was it just because of the fight, or did he have something else to feel guilty about? What could he have done to upset Jill so much, and why was he so secretive about it? Maybe there was a link between this incident and the mix-up inside the vault. Nancy made a mental note to follow up on the incident.

"When you're done with that, Maurice," Mr. Charles added, "I have two new teller trainees for you, Bess Marvin and George Fayne." He pointed to the girls, who were standing on the other side of the partition.

Maurice looked up over his shoulder at Bess and George. "Yes, sir," he told Mr. Charles with a nod.

"And this is our new intern, Nancy Drew. I was just in the middle of giving her a tour when your . . . disagreement interrupted us." Mr. Charles's tone was disapproving. "Come on, Nancy. Let's hope we're not interrupted again." Still looking angry, Mr. Charles turned his back on Maurice and led Nancy out.

"So you've begun your work here with a bang," he

12

said as he and Nancy walked over to the staircase. Nancy was glad he'd used the word *work* instead of investigation. Sound seemed to travel in the bank, and a lot of people were around to hear. In fact Nancy was quickly getting the feeling that this was a very difficult place in which to keep a secret—even though there seemed to be plenty of them.

"Whoever said banks were quiet and sedate never was in *this* one," she quipped.

Mr. Charles smiled but his brow wrinkled, showing how upset he really was. "Well, they *ought* to be quiet."

Nancy lowered her voice as they reached the curved marble staircase that led to the basement. "I'll make sure it gets back to being that way." She grasped the polished brass banister as they hurried past an electric eye. It beeped as they stepped in front of it. "I've got to tell you, I'm no expert on bank security," she commented. "How is the vault set up?"

"It's pretty simple," Mr. Charles answered, "and it's so secure I can't believe anyone actually got in. There's only one way to get down to the basement—this staircase. At the bottom of the steps there's a gate leading to the security desk. A guard is posted there nine A.M. to five P.M. Then there's another gate. You need a special key to get through it." He jangled his overloaded key ring. "Behind that is the vault. Inside it, a video camera keeps twenty-four-hour security."

The end of the stairway's curve gave Nancy her first view of the vault. Behind the first gate a gray-haired man in a blue uniform sat behind a high mahogany desk. He was lean and muscular, a fit sixty years old. When he saw Mr. Charles and Nancy, he hopped out of his seat and hurried over to open the gate. As soon as

13

they entered the small area, he closed and locked the gate behind them.

"Nancy, I'd like you to meet Larry Jaye, our vault attendant. Larry, this is Nancy Drew. She's going to be an intern here."

Larry gave Nancy a friendly smile and shook her hand. "Welcome!" he said warmly. "You sure did pick the right bank to intern in, young lady. We've got the nicest people I've seen anywhere. And I bet you'll learn a whole lot from Mr. Charles. He may be young, but he knows everything about banking from his daddy and his daddy before him—"

"Uh . . . Larry," Mr. Charles interrupted, looking embarrassed. "I've brought Nancy down here to show her how the vault works. Would you be kind enough to help me?"

"Why, sure," Larry agreed. He pushed a thick bound notebook toward them. Nancy saw that the book was open to a page with a list of signatures on it. "You know I'm going to have to ask you to sign this," he said, nodding to Mr. Charles as if they'd been through this countless times before. "You may be the president and all, but rules are rules."

Mr. Charles smiled as he signed his name. *"Everybody* signs," he explained to Nancy, handing her the pen. "It's one of our many security precautions. That way we know everyone who enters or leaves the vault."

Nancy quickly pulled out her notepad and jotted down a reminder to check the names in the book later. Then she signed her own name in the security log. Mr. Charles used a cylinder key to unlock the second steel gate. Behind it was a steel wall with a huge metal door in the middle of it. The door stood open, and as she stepped through it, Nancy judged it to be about two feet thick.

"This here's our vault," Larry said, with a touch of pride.

He gave the door a gentle tap, and it swung smoothly and silently until it was almost all the way closed. Larry stopped it with two fingers before it shut completely. "You'd never believe this door weighs as much as it does," he said. "Moves just like a feather."

Nancy stepped to the door, tapping the metal wheel on the front. "Is that a combination lock?" she asked.

"You got it," Larry confirmed.

"So to open the vault, you just have to know the combination?"

It was Mr. Charles who answered her. "No," he said. "You need a second person to turn off the alarm."

Mr. Charles pointed to a small metal pane next to the vault door, with numbered buttons set up in a grid, like on a push-button phone.

"You have to punch a special numerical code to disarm the alarm," he told Nancy. "If the code isn't entered within one minute of unlocking the vault, an alarm sounds and the police get over here fast."

"Let me get this straight," Nancy said. "To break in, you'd need to get past the cameras and the guards in the lobby, have the key to both the first *and* the second gates, then use the special codes to unlock the vault and turn off the alarm?"

"Right," said Mr. Charles. "And nobody knows both the code to the vault and the code to turn off the alarm. Not even me. That way, no one person can open the vault alone," he explained. "We call it the dual control system."

"Keeps everybody honest," Larry agreed.

"You'd think with all that security it would be impossible to break in," Nancy said. "So who knows the door combination?"

15

"I do," said Larry.

"And just one other person," Mr. Charles added. "Our assistant branch manager, Evelyn Sobel."

"And who knows the alarm code?" Nancy asked.

"I do," Mr. Charles replied. "And Maurice Grun, our head teller."

"Hmm," Nancy murmured thoughtfully. That piece of information made her even more suspicious of Maurice than the commotion upstairs had. So Maurice knew the alarm code. If he was working with someone who knew the door combination—either Larry Jaye or Evelyn Sobel—he'd have access to the vault. Of course, that didn't explain how he could have gotten the safe-deposit boxes open. Nancy remembered he'd need both the bank's and the customer's key. But at least she had a theory.

"Larry, will you excuse us, please?" Mr. Charles asked. "I'm going to take Nancy inside the vault."

"Yes, sir, Mr. Charles," said Larry, hurrying back to his desk. "Nice to meet you, young lady."

Nancy smiled at the guard as she followed Mr. Charles into the vault. Larry Jaye certainly seemed like a nice person. She hoped he wasn't one of the people involved with the break-in. She'd have to meet this Evelyn Sobel as soon as she could.

Once inside, Nancy gazed around her at the scene of the crime—or the future crime! The two side walls were covered with hundreds of steel drawers of different sizes, and more boxes flanked the vault's door. Even the ceiling was steel, with naked light bulbs hanging down from it at regular intervals. The vault's floor was made out of the same solid white marble as the rest of the bank's. In the rear wall, also made of steel, were three doors.

"What's behind the doors?" Nancy inquired.

16

"Those are cubicles where box holders can view their belongings in private," Mr. Charles explained. Once again he pulled out his key ring, then opened the middle cubicle. The small room was wood paneled, with a wooden counter and a single chair. "In here, customers have complete privacy. Unless they choose to tell us, we have absolutely no idea what they keep inside their boxes."

"So there could be almost *anything* inside these boxes," Nancy said.

"That's right," Mr. Charles answered. He and Nancy stepped out of the room, and he relocked the door. "By the way, smile for the camera." He pointed at a security eye mounted near the ceiling.

Nancy took a good, hard look at the camera, encased in its black metal box. It looked invulnerable. "So somehow they opened that up and erased the video-tape?" Nancy asked.

"Yes, and I have no more idea of how they did that than how they got through the locked doors and special codes," Mr. Charles said. "Oh, and Nancy, our vault has one more special feature. If it's opened at any time other than during normal business hours, the door is set to remain open just five minutes. After that, the alarm goes off and the door slams shut."

Nancy pulled out her notepad and pen and began to write. There was a lot of information she didn't want to forget. She didn't get very far with her notes, though, because suddenly Elaine Kussack, Mr. Charles's secretary, came rushing into the vault, breathless.

"Mr. Charles!" she cried. "I'm so sorry! I just can't believe it!"

"What's the matter, Elaine?" asked Mr. Charles.

Before she could answer, Larry Jaye came rushing in after her, carrying the leather notebook. "Now, you

17

wait just one minute, ma'am!" he shouted, waving a pen. "*Nobody* gets inside this vault without signing in." Larry turned to Mr. Charles. "I tried to stop her, Mr. Charles, but when I unlocked the gate, she just barged through." He glared at Elaine Kussack.

"That's fine," Mr. Charles said, taking the notebook and signing Ms. Kussack's name quickly, but all his attention was on his secretary. "Now tell me what happened."

"Oh, Mr. Charles, I'm so sorry," Ms. Kussack sobbed. "I should have been there to stop it."

"Stop what?" Mr. Charles asked, his face growing worried.

"Mr. Charles," she said, her voice shaking, "your office has just been robbed!"

3

The Telltale Glove

"A robbery!" Mr. Charles gasped. He shot Nancy a worried look. But in the next instant he switched his tone back to the cool, professional one Nancy had grown used to hearing. "Don't worry, Elaine," he said reassuringly. "I'm sure it wasn't your fault. Let's go upstairs and find out exactly what happened."

Nancy had to admire Alan Charles. Letting his own worries show would have been a very bad thing for the bank just then, and he had covered up admirably. What's more, he was smoothly getting her and Elaine away from the guard in order to discuss the break-in.

Taking his secretary's arm, Mr. Charles steered her out of the vault. Nancy followed him past the guard's desk.

"Uh, excuse me, Mr. Charles, sir," Larry called after them. "Hate to bother you."

"Yes?" Mr. Charles turned, a slightly impatient edge to his voice.

Larry pushed the leather-bound notebook across the

desk toward them. "Rules are rules," he said with an embarrassed smile, "and all of you have to sign out."

Mr. Charles signed the book quickly, followed by Ms. Kussack. As Nancy followed suit, she couldn't help but notice Larry's care with his work. After all, the safeguards needed to be followed in order to keep the vault secure. They had to be completed, even during an emergency.

Larry opened the outer gate, then locked it once more after they'd passed to the other side.

Nancy hurried up the curved staircase with the bank president and his secretary. "Don't say a word about this until we get to my office," Mr. Charles instructed them. "Sound really carries in this place, and it's absolutely necessary that no one besides us knows about this."

As the stairway opened out into the lobby, Nancy took a quick look around. Everything seemed to be calm. Nothing was out of place, either, as they went up the next flight of steps, nor as they sped down the long hallway and into Ms. Kussack's office.

The secretary's office looked neat enough, but Nancy was sure the real damage lay behind the closed door of Mr. Charles's office. Nancy turned and shut the outer door firmly behind them.

As the door clicked shut, Elaine Kussack burst out, "It's awful, just awful!" Nancy noticed that her hands were shaking. "I was gone less than ten minutes. I just went to the coffee shop for our usual morning dough-nuts. Before I left, I locked your door and my door, the way I always do. When I got back, both doors were wide open—and I saw this!" She flung open the heavy mahogany door to Mr. Charles's office.

Mr. Charles gasped and Nancy's eyes widened at what they saw. The whole room was a mess. Papers

20

were scattered all over the floor. A few of Mr. Charles's family pictures had been tossed from the wall and lay on the ground, surrounded by broken glass from the frames. The drawers of the desk had been wrenched from their places, but the papers in them hadn't been dumped out. They remained neatly filed, as Mr. Charles had left them.

Worst of all, in the center of the wall behind the desk, a safe stood exposed to view, its supposedly impenetrable door wide open. Nancy hadn't noticed the safe when she'd been in Mr. Charles's office earlier, so she assumed it had been hidden behind one of the pictures that were now scattered on the floor.

"Oh no!" Mr. Charles cried, running to the safe. He stuck his head inside, peering carefully at its contents, taking account of what might be stolen.

Nancy hurried around his desk to get a better look. "What's missing?" she asked.

Mr. Charles pulled his head out of the safe, a perplexed expression on his face. "Nothing!" he exclaimed.

"How strange," Nancy commented. "Why go to all the trouble of breaking in here when you don't intend to take anything?"

"That's not the only strange thing," Mr. Charles said. "The duplicate keys to the safe-deposit boxes— the ones I said were missing? Well, they're back! Obviously the thief—" Abruptly, Mr. Charles interrupted himself. Turning to his secretary, he asked, "Elaine, would you do me a big favor?"

"Of course, Mr. Charles."

"My nerves are pretty frayed right now. Would you run to the drugstore and get me some extra-strength aspirin?" He took out his wallet and handed her a five-dollar bill.

21

"I'd be happy to," Ms. Kussack said, and headed for the door.

"Oh, and Elaine, do me an even bigger favor. Don't mention this to anyone."

The secretary nodded at him understandingly. "I'll be right back."

"That was wise," Nancy told Mr. Charles. "The less anyone else knows about this, the better—even someone whom you trust, like Ms. Kussack."

"It's awful having to be suspicious of everyone, but I guess that's what we've got to do." Mr. Charles sighed.

Nancy nodded. "You know," she said slowly, "none of this makes any sense. The thief must have stolen the duplicate keys much earlier in order to get into the vault the other night. So why go to all the trouble of breaking in a second time to put them back? What's more," she continued, "the thief ran a big risk coming in here in the middle of the day. . . . But what was it Ms. Kussack said about your usual morning doughnuts?"

Charles smiled ruefully. "It's a little ritual we have. Every morning around this time, Elaine goes down and gets us each a glazed jelly doughnut."

"That could explain why the thief took the risk," Nancy cut in. "If someone knew your secretary's schedule and then saw you go downstairs, it would have been clear that your office was empty—a perfect time to break in. Which reinforces your theory that it's an inside job."

"At least the keys are back where they belong," said Mr. Charles. The worry lines eased from his face just a little.

"But that doesn't mean your troubles are over," Nancy cautioned. "The thief could have made copies. Anyway, we still have a few questions to answer. Like, why break in twice? And how did the thief get through the two locks—on your door and Ms. Kussack's?"

She glanced at the entry to his office, then walked over to examine the doorknob. The lock's shiny metal was unscratched—no signs of tampering. A quick perusal of Ms. Kussack's door showed a similar lack of marks.

"The thief must have had a key, to get in and out so fast," Nancy said as she reentered the bank president's office.

"But that's impossible," Mr. Charles said. "Elaine and I are the only ones with keys. And I'll show you something else that's impossible." Mr. Charles pointed to the door of the wall safe. "This lock wasn't forced open, it was picked!"

"I don't want to sound unsympathetic," Nancy told him, "but a combination lock is all too easy to pick. It happens all the time. And if the culprit could break into the vault, wouldn't a small safe like this be relatively simple?"

"No," said Mr. Charles. "It would be a lot harder. You see, there are four people, including me, who could get into the vault. But I'm the *only* person who knows the combination to this safe. And the combination is so long and complicated, it would take even a master safecracker several hours to figure it out."

Nancy tapped her fingers on the dark mahogany of Mr. Charles's desk, thinking hard. There were just too many "impossibles" in this case. "So all we can really assume," she concluded, "is that this *is* an inside job, given how quickly the robbery was done, and that the thief knew when you and Ms. Kussack would be out. But it seems our intruder also has magical abilities to open doors without keys and locks without combinations."

23

"And we still don't know what this person is after," Mr. Charles added.

"Is anything else missing from your office?" Nancy asked.

Mr. Charles checked through the open drawers. Then he gathered the papers from the floor and quickly shuffled through them. "I think everything's here," he said finally, "though I'll have to sort through all this stuff before I'm certain. It seems like whoever was here just wanted to make a mess." Mr. Charles dropped tiredly to the brown upholstered armchair behind his desk. "At least, I *hope* that was all they wanted."

"It *can't* be all," Nancy said. "No one goes to so much trouble for essentially nothing."

Mr. Charles shook his head. "I know. But since technically there still hasn't been a robbery, I'm not going to alert the police. Some nosy reporter over at the *Bentley Times* would get wind of this so fast, they'd have a banner headline about it in tonight's paper. Then my customers would bring wheelbarrows to cart their money out of here."

Nancy was barely listening as her keen blue eyes glanced around the room. "There *has* to be a clue," she said. "Too much has happened already for there not to be *something*."

"I'm giving you free run of the office," Mr. Charles told her. "At a time like this, I can't afford to keep anything from you. If you need me, I'll be at Elaine's desk." Mr. Charles rose from his chair, and Nancy noticed his shoulders drooping as he disappeared into the adjoining office.

Alone, Nancy walked over to the open wall safe. She was glad Mr. Charles trusted her with the important papers and keys involved in running the bank. If he

24

held back with her, the case really would be impossible to solve. She peered curiously into the safe. In it, a large key ring rested on top of a neat pile of papers. The papers hadn't been touched—Nancy could tell because the edges of the pages lined up exactly. A thief in a hurry would never have taken the time to reassemble them like that. Picking up the ring, she saw that every key had a small number etched into it. She guessed that each one corresponded to a different safe-deposit box in the vault.

Well, the safe didn't appear to hold any secrets—at least not the kind that would help her solve the mystery. Maybe she'd have better luck with the drawers. But as she started going through the files, Nancy realized that they were also a dead end. They hadn't been disturbed.

But there *had* to be a clue somewhere. Nancy knew that criminals made mistakes. Sighing, she got down on her hands and knees. Maybe there was something on the floor, some paper or scrap that would provide a key to this strange mystery.

She couldn't see too clearly in the shadows, but a small, dark object lay crumpled on the white marble floor. Reaching for it, Nancy felt something soft and smooth, like leather. Inching the object toward her, she pulled out a brown glove.

She sat up, leaning back on her heels. It was a woman's right-hand glove, unusually small, and it had the letter *S* embroidered across the back of it in brown thread. Had the intruder worn this to avoid leaving fingerprints?

Nancy's mind clicked away as it processed the information this first clue gave her. If this *was* the thief's glove, then that person was a right-handed woman with a small hand and at least one initial *S*. The initial knocked out all her suspects—except one. Evelyn Sobel, the only person besides Larry Jaye who knew the combination to the vault.

But maybe someone else had left the glove, someone uninvolved in the robbery, someone Mr. Charles had legitimate business with. Nancy scrambled to her feet and ran to the outer office.

"Have you found something?" Mr. Charles asked excitedly.

"Maybe you can tell me," Nancy responded. "Have you ever seen this before?" She held out the glove.

Mr. Charles took the soft leather, examining it carefully, then shook his head.

"Has anybody been in your office recently? Anyone with the initial S?"

Mr. Charles thought a moment. "I don't usually have anyone up here except Elaine. When I meet with my managers, it's usually in the conference room down the hall. So I guess the answer is no."

"Then this is our first clue," Nancy replied, retrieving the glove from Mr. Charles. A small smile spread across her face. She was sure this one would lead to a second, a third, and finally to a solution. "By the way, I ought to get out of here before Ms. Kussack gets back with your aspirin. She's probably already wondering what an intern like me is doing spending so much time with the boss. I don't want to blow my cover."

"I wouldn't worry," said Mr. Charles. "Elaine is very discreet. That's one of the reasons I hired her when dad's old secretary, Rita, retired six months ago."

Nancy smiled. "It's good at least something at the bank is going right." She tapped the glove. "And now something is going right with this case." She stashed her first clue in her purse, then turned to leave. "I

26

guess I'll go check on Bess and George. Maybe they've learned something more."

Mr. Charles nodded. "If you need any help or information, you know where I am."

Half an hour later Nancy, Bess, and George sat lunching at Kathy's, a sidewalk café in the middle of Bentley's quaint downtown area. A cheery green-and-white-striped awning shielded them from the midday sun, and the view of the marina with the lake beyond it couldn't be beat. Nancy settled comfortably into the green-and-white-striped cushion of her chair. All in all, it had been an interesting morning.

"Maurice told us this is where all the bank employees hang out," Bess said, biting into her pizza burger and reaching for a french fry at the same time. "So maybe we'll pick up a clue or two while we eat. That's my kind of detective work!" She let out a giggle.

George made a face as she watched her cousin. "How can you eat that stuff?" she asked. "Do you realize how much fat and cholesterol is in there?"

Bess shrugged. "I worked hard this morning," she said. "Counting money burns a lot of calories."

"What else did Maurice tell you?" Nancy asked her friends.

George took a bite of her spinach salad. "Well, the very first thing we learned is the Bentley Bank motto." Bess chimed in as George recited, "At Bentley Bank, our goal is to serve *you*.

"Other than that, it was just a lot of stuff about bank procedure," George added. "You know, how to take a deposit, how to issue a withdrawal. And lots of rules and regulations."

Bess put down her pizza burger long enough to pull a

27

thick packet of papers out of her bag. Dropping it on the table, she said, "This is the tellers' training manual. Can you believe we have to read all this? You definitely got the better job."

Nancy smiled, but she was too intent on questioning her friends to respond to Bess's joke. "Were you able to find out anything more about what happened this morning with that girl Jill?" she asked. "It's just possible that the fight ties in with the break-ins."

"I asked Maurice about that," George agreed with a nod, "but he wouldn't say a word. He seemed really nervous, though, all morning. And he left us a couple of times—to make phone calls, he said." Nancy picked absentmindedly at her tuna-fish sandwich as she listened to her friend.

"What's it all about?" George wondered. "Have *you* learned anything?"

Nancy reviewed the details she'd gathered so far: the break-in in the vault and the one in Mr. Charles's office, the "dual control" system to enter the vault, and the small leather right-handed glove.

"I think we can safely say it's an inside job," Nancy concluded. "But other than that, there's still not much to go on."

"What *I* want to know," said Bess, "is why someone would go to all the trouble of breaking into the basement vault and then not steal anything. Especially with all that jewelry!"

"There's just one way to explain it," Nancy said, and her eyes seemed fired with determination as she spoke. "They're looking for something more valuable to them than jewelry. Since they haven't found it yet, we know one thing for sure. They'll be back!"

4

Dead End

The idea had come to Nancy in a flash. Something more valuable than jewelry! That *had* to be the answer.

Bess dropped her pizza burger back on her plate in surprise. "What could possibly be more valuable than diamonds and rubies?" she wondered. Then, quick to recover her appetite, she reached for the fries. "Well, at least you know the thief isn't a woman."

Nancy turned to face Bess, puzzled. "Why do you say that?"

"Do you honestly think a woman would pass up all those jewels?"

Nancy frowned. Bess thought *all* women were into the same things she was. "Actually, I think the intruder probably *is* a woman," Nancy told her friends. "Or at least one of them is."

"Why do you say that?" George asked.

Nancy pulled the glove from her pocket and held it out in the palm of her hand. "It's so small," she said. "I seriously doubt a man's hand would fit into it."

Bess reached out to take it, and in a single movement tried unsuccessfully to pull the glove over the short, plump fingers of her right hand. "Even *my* hand won't fit in it," she commented. "And I'm really small-boned."

"I can't say who is the owner of that glove," Nancy commented, "though Evelyn Sobel came instantly to mind when I saw that *S.* But there might be other possibilities." Nancy pushed back her chair and stood up, glancing at her barely touched sandwich. She didn't have time to finish it now—the mystery was just beginning to heat up. "If you two are done with lunch, let's get back to the bank," she said. "We have some clues to follow."

A few minutes later Nancy was back in Mr. Charles's office, staring over his shoulder and into the glow of his computer monitor. Luckily, Ms. Kussack was out on her lunch break, which gave Nancy the perfect chance to check files without putting her cover identity in danger.

"This will just take a second," Mr. Charles said. He tapped on a floor switch with the toe of his shoe. A second later the computer beeped and a menu appeared on the screen. Mr. Charles hit a few keys with his index finger and a list of names appeared.

Nancy scanned the list, her eyes peeled for the letter *S.* There were several Susans, a Sarah, and one Sylvester. She wrote each one down in her notebook. Then her gaze traveled down the last names. She jotted down each one that began with an *S.* She triple underlined one in particular. Evelyn Sobel, the assistant branch manager.

"I'd like to take down a few addresses," Nancy told Mr. Charles, "in case I need to track someone down after banking hours."

"Of course," Mr. Charles said.

Nancy jotted down Evelyn Sobel's address as well as those of Larry and Maurice. That covered everyone who knew the combination to either the vault or the alarm. "There's just one more I need," she said. "What's Jill's last name—you know, the girl who stormed out of here this morning?"

"Adler," Mr. Charles said.

Nancy found Jill's address. "Sixty-four Mountain Avenue," Nancy murmured, writing it down. Then she snapped the notebook shut. "I'm going to pay Ms. Adler a visit, to try to find out what that blow-up was all about."

"Mountain Avenue's just a few blocks from here," Mr. Charles told her, and he gave her some quick directions.

"In that case, I'll walk," Nancy said.

Nancy knew she had to talk to Bess and George before she left, so she made a point to stop in the lobby. Bess was working with a customer, but George was over by the photocopy machine making copies from a thick three-ring binder. Checking first to make sure none of the other bank employees were within earshot—and hoping they wouldn't notice the two of them talking— Nancy hurried over.

George grinned as she saw Nancy, then rolled her eyes. "I'm copying all the bank transactions for the past month. Let me tell you, working at a bank can be really boring sometimes."

"Well, I've got an assignment for you," Nancy whispered, "so maybe that will liven things up."

George smiled. "At Bentley Bank, our goal is to serve *you*."

Nancy laughed, then said, "In connection with the glove, keep your eyes open for Evelyn Sobel."

"Anything specific you want us to find out?"

"Whatever you can," Nancy said. "And while you're at it, take a look at her hands. Those gloves were pretty small."

"Got it," George said.

Nancy gave her friend's hand a squeeze, then started across the lobby. Pushing open one of the big wooden doors, she emerged into the afternoon sunlight. A fresh summer breeze was blowing up the hill from Lake Bentley. Closing her eyes, Nancy let the cool wind tickle her neck, and she lifted her face to catch the warmth of the sun. It was such a beautiful day. Too bad she didn't have time to enjoy it.

Nancy shook her head. She needed to concentrate on the task at hand. As she followed Mr. Charles's directions past the police station, Kathy's Café, and Bentley Hospital, she couldn't help wondering what she was walking into. After all, she already knew Jill Adler had a very nasty temper.

Turning onto Mountain Avenue, Nancy saw that it was extremely steep. She peered down the hill, saw a dead end, and at the bottom, a tall metal barricade. Beyond it, Lake Bentley sparkled in the sun. The street was so narrow that there wasn't even a sidewalk, and the rows of parked cars that lined both sides of the pavement were squeezed up against the high hedges of the houses. Nancy started down the slope, walking in the middle of the quiet street.

As she walked, she went over what she knew so far. At least two criminals had to be working together to get inside the vault. Larry Jaye and Evelyn Sobel were the only ones who knew the vault combination. Mr. Charles and Maurice Grun knew the alarm code. One person from each pair had to be in on the job.

It was pretty unlikely that Mr. Charles would undermine his own business, and besides, he was the one who had called her in on the job. So the criminal who knew the alarm code had to be Maurice Grun. Now the question was, who was he working with, Evelyn Sobel or Larry Jaye? And was anyone else in on the crime—like Jill Adler?

The sound of a motor interrupted Nancy's thoughts. Turning, she saw the front end of a car as it pulled off a side street and paused at the corner of Mountain Avenue. Nancy checked the numbers of the house nearest to her. Number 64, Jill's house, must be down at the bottom of the hill.

The question was, how did Jill fit into the puzzle? She didn't have access to the vault. Still, Nancy couldn't rule her out as a suspect. Maybe she had other information the thieves needed. Without knowing what her fight with Maurice had been about, Nancy guessed that the two had a close relationship. Whether their connection was personal or criminal, Nancy wasn't sure. But she needed to find out.

The slope took an even steeper dip as Nancy neared the bottom of the hill. The metal barrier was just a few yards ahead of her. She took a deep breath as she stepped toward the last house on the right, number 64, a well-tended two-family home.

Before Nancy could reach the door, the sound of a car motor cut into the serene afternoon. Nancy turned to glance over her shoulder at the noise, then froze in horror. The car she'd seen above her on the hill was racing down Mountain Avenue straight toward her. In another instant it would send her slamming fatally into the metal fence!

Nancy looked frantically to her right and left. She

was hemmed in on either side by parked cars, and there was nothing but the ten-foot-high metal barricade directly ahead of her. With nowhere to turn, she had time for only one shocking realization. The car had no driver!

5

A Broken Engagement

Escape was impossible! Nancy hadn't an inch to spare, and in a few seconds the driverless car would come crashing onto her!

Reacting with pure instinct, she leapt to her right. She could feel her back come slamming down onto something metal—the hood of a parked car. Rolling over it, she slid across the hedge and dropped down to the private lawn on the other side. The moment she landed, she heard a deafening boom and felt a rush of heat as the car exploded.

For a moment Nancy lay still, her ears ringing with the noise, her heart pounding. Then, taking a deep breath, she grabbed the scratchy branches of the bush and cautiously pulled herself to her feet.

The explosion of light from the fire was so intense that she had to shield her eyes from it. The black outline of the driverless car was still visible inside the bonfire of orange flames that rose high into the air. The sweet-smelling lake breeze was now sooty with smoke.

Nancy shuddered. To think that she had almost been caught in the middle of it all! Taking a slow, deep breath, she checked herself over. Luckily, she hadn't suffered anything worse than a few bruises and some grass stains on her blue suit.

She was sure it was no accident that a driverless car had suddenly taken off like a missile down the very street on which she'd been walking. Someone wanted her dead! And that someone had probably seen her leave the bank, followed in the car, and jumped out just before it crashed!

Nancy scanned the hill, although she was certain the would-be murderer had long since escaped. Sure enough, the only people she saw were coming out of their houses to check out the terrible fire. Nancy frowned, feeling shaken and angry. She didn't know who the driver had been. She had, however, learned an important fact about the suspects. They might not have committed a robbery—yet—but they certainly weren't above committing murder!

"Are you all right?" a woman called out.

Nancy turned. The upstairs door to 64 Mountain Avenue had been thrown wide open. Jill Adler was running down the exterior staircase and across the lawn toward her. An expression of fear and concern gripped the petite girl's pretty features, and her dark hair bounced as she ran.

Though still dazed, Nancy realized this was a lucky break. Now she had the perfect excuse to talk to Jill.

"I'm fine," she reassured Jill, "but I think I'd better sit down for a moment—and someone needs to call the fire department. Would it be okay if I used your phone?"

"Oh sure," Jill agreed readily. "Come on up."

Nancy followed Jill toward the shingled white

house. There was a front door at street level, and stairs ran up the side of the house to another door on the second floor. Jill headed up the flight of stairs, with Nancy close behind her.

As Nancy stepped inside, she found herself in a small living room with a faded flowered sofa and chair with saggy cushions. The telephone sat atop an old oversize TV that was set into a fake wood cabinet.

Jill seemed a little embarrassed about the decor. "The furniture used to belong to my parents," she explained apologetically. "They unloaded it on me when they got their new living room set."

"It's fine," Nancy reassured her with a smile.

"Why don't you sit down and relax a bit while I call the fire department and the police," Jill suggested. "I'm sure you don't feel up to much right now."

"Thanks," Nancy said. As she sank into the chair's soft cushions, she realized she was more tired than she thought. She appreciated Jill's consideration at this moment. Could this really be the same person who'd thrown the money trays around the bank that morning?

Jill handled the emergency calls in a straightforward, clear manner, and Nancy found herself actually liking her suspect—especially after Jill hung up the phone and hurried to get her a tall glass of orange juice.

When Jill settled into the flowered sofa across from Nancy's chair, Nancy noticed that Jill's eyes were red and puffy, as if she'd been crying.

"You look like you haven't had a much better day than I have," Nancy said sympathetically.

Jill shrugged. "I just quit my job."

"I know," Nancy said. "In fact, that's why I was coming to see you, believe it or not."

37

Jill looked at her suspiciously. "Who are you?" she demanded, her friendliness vanishing instantly.

Nancy had already figured out a story to explain her presence. It wasn't *too* much of a lie, but she couldn't be sure that Jill would buy it.

"I'm Nancy Drew," she began. "I'm a new intern over at the bank. Mr. Charles asked me to come over here to make sure you're all right. We were all pretty concerned about you this morning."

Jill laughed without humor. "Not *all* of you," she replied bitterly. "I know one particular bank employee who isn't the least bit concerned. In fact, if it hadn't been for him, I'd still have a job right now."

Nancy chose her words carefully. "I realize we don't know each other, but if you feel like talking about it, I'm a good listener. Maybe I could even talk to Mr. Charles and help you get your job back."

"For an intern you seem to have a lot of clout with the boss," Jill commented suspiciously.

Nancy silently chastised herself. If she didn't watch it, she'd have no cover left by the time she finished with Jill. But her own worries turned to genuine concern for Jill when she saw the other girl's expression crumble and big, wet tears begin snaking down her cheeks. Jill buried her face in her hands and great, heaving sobs racked her whole body. Nancy rummaged through her purse, looking for a tissue. She came up with a clean, slightly rumpled one.

"Here," she said, holding the tissue out to Jill. Jill took it and blew her nose. "Is there something I can do?" Nancy asked. "Really, I'd like to help."

Jill didn't answer, but soon she began to cry more softly. Then she wiped her eyes and took a deep breath.

"I might as well tell you the whole story," she said.

"Sometimes it's easier talking to someone you don't know."

"Who are you upset with?" Nancy asked, not letting on how much she knew.

"His name is Maurice Grun," Jill said with a sigh. She picked nervously at the frayed upholstery of the sofa. "When I woke up this morning, I wasn't upset with him at all. In fact, I was engaged to him. We were supposed to be married next month. But today, as soon as I got to work, he came up to my station and said, 'It's over. I'd like the ring back.'"

"Just like that?" Nancy asked incredulously. "Didn't he give you any explanation?"

Jill nodded sadly. "He said he'd met someone else. As simple as that. I just couldn't believe it. I kept staring at him, thinking it was some kind of cruel joke. Then I realized he meant it, and I exploded! I don't think I've ever been so angry in my entire life. How could he have done this to me? How could he tell me he loved me one minute, then go behind my back the next? If I ever get my hands on him, I'll—" Jill broke off as she began to sob again.

Moving over to the couch, Nancy put a comforting arm around the other girl's shoulder. "I'm so sorry," she said.

After a few moments Jill calmed down. "It's probably good I found out he's a rat *before* I married him." She wiped a smudge of makeup from under one eye. "Anyway, at least we don't have to sneak around anymore."

"Why did you have to sneak around in the first place?" Nancy asked.

"Well, technically, we were breaking the rules," Jill replied.

Before Nancy had time to ask what Jill was talking

about, she heard the wail of police sirens and fire engines. Jill sat up straight, looking startled.

"What's the matter?" Nancy asked as the alarms grew louder.

Jill didn't say anything right away. After a moment she relaxed and sank back into the sofa cushion. "It's nothing," she whispered. "Just the loud noise. They're here for the fire."

But Jill's reaction didn't make sense to Nancy. Maybe Jill was afraid of more than just the sirens, Nancy thought. "What did you mean, you and Maurice were breaking the rules?"

"Since you just started, you probably don't know this," Jill began, "but the bank has a rule against employees being married to each other, so Maurice and I had to keep our engagement a secret."

"Why do they have that rule?" Nancy asked.

"If two bank employees have a close relationship," Jill explained, "they might share confidential information. Not that Maurice and I would ever do something like that. We were just in love. At least I thought we were."

For a moment Nancy was afraid Jill was going to break down and start crying again.

"You should have seen the ring he gave me," she continued. "It was so *huge*, like something out of a dream."

"How big *was* it?" Nancy asked.

"Five carats."

Nancy whistled. "That *is* huge. But it must have cost a fortune. How could Maurice have afforded it? He couldn't make that much money as head teller."

"I was wondering the same thing," Jill admitted. "I asked him about it, but he just told me not to worry. He said he wanted to cover me in jewels, that he could . . .

40

that he *would*. Not that I'm ever going to see any of them now." Tears began to fill Jill's brown eyes, but she brushed them away.

Nancy couldn't help wondering how Maurice had intended to make good on his boast. Had he been thinking of all the jewelry inside the vault? Where had he gotten the money for even the one diamond ring? Mr. Charles had said nothing was missing from the safe-deposit boxes, but maybe he was wrong. Maybe a ring *had* been taken, but the owners hadn't discovered it yet!

Nancy licked her lips as she reviewed the possibilities. Maurice knew the vault combination. If he was working with someone who knew the alarm code— Evelyn or Larry—then a lovely ring for his fiancée would have been easy to get. It was time to get to work on the secondary suspects. Next stop, Evelyn Sobel's office!

But Nancy didn't want to arouse Jill's suspicion. Trying to look natural, she checked her watch. "Oh, wow, it's really gotten late. I should be getting back to work," she said, standing. "I wish there was something more I could do for you. Would you like me to talk to Mr. Charles about giving you your job back?"

Jill shook her head adamantly. "There's no way I'd go back there now. I don't think I could bear to face Maurice after what he did." Jill attempted a wan smile, then added, "But thanks for being so nice. You were right. You *are* a very good listener."

"What will you do?" Nancy asked, genuinely concerned.

Jill let out her first real smile since Nancy had met her. "I was already looking for another job, anyway. I was pretty tired of working at the bank. I'll find something."

41

Nancy patted Jill's shoulder. "Good luck. And thanks for helping me after the accident."

When Nancy stepped outside Jill's door, fire fighters in black rubber raincoats were still hosing down the twisted, charred metal that had once been a car. Three fire trucks were parked one behind the other, and in back of them, two police cars flashed their red warning signals. A crowd of curious neighbors bombarded the officers with questions.

Nancy was sure the police would love to question her about the accident, but she didn't want to get involved with them yet. She'd have to explain too much about the situation at the bank, and she'd promised Mr. Charles to keep that information confidential. She was fairly sure no one had actually seen her part in the accident, so she hoped she could just slip away quietly.

As she threaded her way around the fire trucks and police cars, she couldn't help feeling sorry for Jill. She really did want to help her, but there was truly nothing she could do about her broken heart. Still, proving Maurice was a crook might help Jill get over him faster.

Nancy turned off Mountain Avenue and walked the few blocks back to the bank. When she arrived, she found Bess and George still behind the tellers' counter, helping customers, and both looking very bored. She'd been hoping to slip quietly through the lobby, but when her friends spotted her, George mouthed the word "wait."

Hmmm, Nancy thought, something must be up—though she hoped it wasn't as drastic as what had happened to her. When George's customer stepped away at last, Nancy slipped over to her window.

"Come back for a second. Bess and I want to tell you something." George's voice was low but excited. "I'll buzz you in."

42

When Nancy entered the tellers' area, Bess hurried over to Nancy and George.

"Come on," Bess whispered, grabbing Nancy's arm and pulling her into a tiny lounge area. "We can't talk long, or Maurice will get on our case," she said, "but you'll never guess what I saw!"

"Does it have to do with Evelyn Sobel?" Nancy asked.

"You must have ESP," Bess answered excitedly. "Wait till you hear this. Remember that right-handed glove you found?" Suddenly Bess fell silent, her blue eyes opened wide, and she wiggled her eyebrows toward her right.

Following Bess's glance, Nancy saw an older woman walking into the lounge. Though her body was small, the woman seemed to command a great deal of strength. Her fluffy gray hair framed a narrow face, and bifocal glasses sat on the bridge of her nose. Dark eyes stared out with a severe expression. Her no-nonsense gray suit completed the picture.

The woman approached them and stopped directly in front of Nancy. "You must be the third new one," she said sternly.

Nancy was startled by the older woman's rude tone.

"Nancy," George said, "I'd like you to meet Evelyn Sobel, assistant branch manager."

Pursing her lips, Ms. Sobel extended her hand to shake Nancy's. "How do you do."

As Nancy took her hand, she instantly realized what Bess and George had been so excited about.

Evelyn Sobel's hand was unusually small. It was just the right size to fit the glove she had found in Mr. Charles's office. The glove with the letter *S!*

6

A Cloud of Smoke

Nancy looked up from Evelyn Sobel's tiny hand to her unfriendly face.

"I can't say I'm pleased to meet you," the branch manager said nastily.

Nancy couldn't believe she'd heard correctly. "Have I done something to offend you?" she asked. "I don't think we've even met."

"Actually, it's not your fault," Ms. Sobel said in a cool, curt voice. "You didn't realize you were breaking protocol by working here."

"I don't understand," Nancy said.

"*I'm* the one who hires all new employees at the bank," Ms. Sobel explained, "yet the three of you have simply appeared out of nowhere."

"Excuse me, Ms. Sobel," Nancy said calmly, "but Mr. Charles hired us this morning."

"He *is* the president," Bess added.

"That doesn't mean he can undermine my authority," Ms. Sobel told them. "I've been here for over twenty-five years. I worked under his father. Mr. Charles was in elementary school when I started here. Now he thinks he can go ahead and hire people without even consulting me? Well, he ought to learn a little respect!"

Then, without even saying goodbye, Ms. Sobel turned and stormed out of the lounge.

"Amazing!" Nancy exclaimed.

"Did you notice her hands?" Bess asked in a whisper. "They look small enough to fit that glove you found."

"Exactly what I was thinking," Nancy agreed. "And I wonder if 'protocol' really was the only reason she was so cold to us. By the way, there have been some developments you two should know about."

Trying not to alarm her friends too much, Nancy explained what she'd learned from Jill Adler. Then she described the near-fatal collision at the bottom of Mountain Avenue.

"Oh, Nancy!" Bess cried, jumping from her chair and hugging her friend. "I can't believe we've been standing here talking calmly when you were almost killed an hour ago!"

"I'm okay," Nancy assured her friend. "But now I really want to figure out who's behind all this—fast!" She pulled out her notepad and glanced through the pages quickly. "Let's see what our complete list of suspects looks like now," she said. "First of all, there's Maurice, who knows the alarm code. Then there are Evelyn and Larry, who know the vault door combination. And Jill might be somewhere in the scenario too."

"Do you think Jill had anything to do with the car crash?" Bess wanted to know.

"Obviously she couldn't have been the driver, since she was in her house," Nancy replied. "But if Maurice

45

planned the crash—and if Jill was involved with him as more than just a fiancée—then she might have known something about it *before* it happened. Of course, I still haven't figured out how any of the suspects could have broken into Mr. Charles's office and safe. To work that quickly, they would have had to have the key and combination, and Mr. Charles swears no one has them but him."

"What I want to know," George said, cutting in, "is what are they after?"

Nancy shrugged. "I can't even guess. But there's *some* good news. After talking to Jill, we know a lot more about Maurice. And his comment about being able to cover Jill in jewels sure makes him sound suspicious."

"You bet it does," Bess agreed. "And what *I* learned about him makes him seem even worse! While you were gone, I tried to get friendly with him, ask him some personal questions—"

"Which is Bess's specialty," George joked.

"I have a gift for communicating with people," Bess said huffily. "Anyway, Maurice mentioned that he'd just gotten engaged to another girl. I tried to get her name, but he wanted real hard to avoid telling me."

"I wonder what his motives were for getting involved in another relationship so quickly," Nancy said. "Maybe he was never really in love with Jill. Maybe he was just using her to get information for the break-in."

"Or maybe this has nothing to do with the bank at all," George volunteered. "It's possible that Maurice just doesn't know which girl he wants."

"Then how do you explain where he got the ring?" Bess asked.

"I can't," George replied with a shrug. "I'm just

saying we still haven't proved Maurice was in the vault. We haven't proved that any of them were."

Nancy flipped through her notes a second time. A reminder she'd written earlier caught her eyes. "Check Larry's book," it said. Hmmm, she'd forgotten about that with all the morning's catastrophes. But now a shiver of excitement snaked its way up her spine. "Hey," she cried. "I've got an easy way to find out exactly who's been in the vault! Anyone who enters or leaves that area has to sign Larry's notebook."

"But they wouldn't sign in if they were robbing the vault," Bess said.

"No," Nancy agreed, "but they wouldn't rob the vault without getting familiar with the layout first. And they'd probably do that during working hours. I think it's time I paid Larry Jaye a visit." With that, Nancy slapped her notepad shut, stuffed it into her purse, and pushed herself out of her chair.

"Be careful, Nancy," Bess said, giving her friend an extra hug. Clearly, she was still very worried about the car crash. George flipped Nancy a thumbs-up sign, and then Nancy made her way out of the room.

The case was complicated, Nancy thought as she stepped across the lobby, then down the stairs and past the electric eye to the vault. But she would sort it out. After all, she'd never failed to solve a case.

The stairway's final turn brought Nancy to the first steel gate. Through the bars she saw the bottom of a pair of men's shoes. They were resting on the surface of the high mahogany desk, their soles scuffed and their heels worn.

The shoes were connected to the blue-trousered legs of Larry Jaye. Nancy could see that the guard's head lolled back in his chair and his eyes were closed. His

47

blue jacket hung on a hook behind him, and his shirt-sleeves were rolled up to the elbows.

Well, it's a good thing there are security gates, she thought as she looked at the dozing guard. Otherwise, all you would have to do to get into the vault would be to tiptoe!

Nancy cleared her throat to get Larry's attention. Immediately the shoes flew off the desk. They landed on the floor with a thud as Larry snapped up in his seat. Then he hurried over to the gate and opened it for her.

"Sign it," he said gruffly, pushing his notebook toward Nancy. "I wasn't sleeping, by the way. Just resting my eyes."

Nancy smiled at Larry's embarrassment. "I don't need to go into the vault," she told him. "I just wanted to bother you with some more intern-type questions."

Larry looked relieved. "Oh, sure," he agreed. "Ask me anything you want." He smiled sheepishly. "I hope you don't think I was goofing off. It just gets so hot and lonely down here in the basement. There hasn't been much traffic through the vault today."

"I understand," said Nancy. She liked Larry. And because of the guard gates, his midday napping didn't seem to bear much on her investigation. "So, anyway, I'm trying to learn a little more about vault procedure." She pointed to the notebook on his desk. "Could I see the log?" she asked. "I never got a good look the last time I was here."

"Go right ahead." Larry turned it back to the first page and held it out to her. "There's nothing much to it, though. Just a lot of names."

Nancy studied the first page. Each line listed the date, a visitor's printed name, the person's signature, the time they signed in, and the time they signed out. The first page was dated about a month earlier. Nancy

48

guessed that previous log books must be stored somewhere else.

As Nancy scanned the notebook page by page, one name kept coming up over and over. Evelyn Sobel! And Nancy began to notice an interesting pattern. Each morning, just after nine o'clock, Ms. Sobel had signed in and then signed out again a few minutes later. Each evening, just before five, she'd signed in and out again. Checking the rest of the pages, Nancy saw that no other bank employee had visited the vault as many times or as regularly.

Ms. Sobel's many visits to the vault would have given her plenty of time to memorize the layout and formulate a plan. Nancy pursed her lips, thinking. It was yet another strike against the unpleasant employee. Ms. Sobel knew the vault door combination. Could she be working with Maurice Grun, who knew the alarm code? Closing the notebook, Nancy pushed it back toward Larry.

"You've seen enough?" he asked.

Nancy nodded. "It's all very interesting," she said. "I never knew there was so much to banking. I thought you just opened an account and that was it."

Larry laughed. "Never gave it much thought, really. Though now that you mention it, I guess there *is* a lot you can do inside a bank."

"Tell me about your job," Nancy encouraged him. "Is it always this quiet?"

Larry nodded. "Pretty much. Not that I mind. It's easy work, and the money's not bad. But sometimes I get so restless down here. I know I look like an old man to you, but I don't feel old inside. I still feel like the wild kid I used to be."

"Where are you from?" Nancy inquired.

"The middle of nowhere," Larry said. "It was such a

no-account hick town, I made myself forget the name."
He laughed.

Nancy studied Larry for a moment. He certainly was in good shape for a man his age. His forearms were muscular with bulging networks of veins. On his right arm, just beneath the elbow, was a faded tattoo. Leaning in a little closer, Nancy saw the tattoo was an intricate drawing of a many-petaled, pale yellow flower. Underneath it was a word Nancy couldn't quite make out.

"Nice tattoo," she said. "It must have taken a real artist to draw something that detailed."

She was about to ask what the word below the flower was when she heard a clattering noise behind her. Nancy turned in time to see a green metal oval bounce down the marble staircase—a hand grenade, she realized with horror!

"Watch out!" Larry shouted.

But before Nancy could act, the grenade's mechanism went off, and a bone-shuddering explosion ripped through the vault.

7

An Unpleasant Encounter

An instant after the grenade went off, Nancy was surprised to find herself still alive. But she was! Her ears stung from the sound of the explosion, and her nose burned with an unusual, bitter smell. Nancy's eyes began to water. Within seconds they felt as if they were on fire, and she jammed them shut to keep out the smoke. Tear gas! she realized. Then the grenade hadn't been meant to kill them after all! Struggling to stay calm, she backed away from the smell and felt for the wall. She knew she had to get out of there, with Larry too, and the staircase was the only way to go.

Flailing out, her hand grazed the steel gate. Nancy knew it was just inches from the steps. Larry hadn't shut it behind her, she remembered. She ran her fingers along the metal bar until she reached the edge. Pushing one foot ahead of her as a guide, she felt for the bottom step.

She heard Larry gasp behind her. "I can't see! Nancy, where are you?"

"I think I'm near the stairs!" she called. "Try to follow my voice." Moving ahead a few inches, she extended her foot again. This time it brushed against the first marble step.

"I found the staircase!" Nancy shouted.

She stumbled on the bottom step, then regained her footing. "Larry, it's this way," she called. As she climbed higher, a cool breeze blew down from the lobby. With each step, she could feel the stinging in her eyes lessen a little, and at last she opened them halfway.

"Nancy?" Larry's gruff voice sounded shaky. "I've reached the first step!"

"Follow me!" Nancy called back. She grasped the curved railing, and they groped their way upward toward the clean air.

A small crowd had gathered at the top of the stairs. Blinking the tears away to clear her eyes, Nancy saw Bess and George trying to push their way forward. In front of them Maurice and Ms. Kussack stood with their arms spread wide to keep everyone away from the steps.

"Please step back!" Ms. Kussack pleaded with the crowd. "Mr. Charles will be here any minute."

"Nancy!" Bess cried from just behind the secretary. "What's that horrible smell?"

Even in her confused state, Nancy realized her friend was making a mistake. No one was supposed to be aware that they had known each other before this morning. Now Bess and George were giving themselves away.

"Are you all right?" George cried, squeezing next to Bess.

An anxious voice called from the crowd, "Is there a fire?"

"Maybe a bomb!" someone else shouted.

"No bomb!" Larry quickly shouted to the crowd, wiping his eyes with a handkerchief. "Just a little problem with the ventilation system. We'll have it working again in no time."

Nancy pressed her lips together, suppressing a smile. She appreciated Larry's quick thinking. His answer had been perfect.

"Everything's all right," Maurice assured the customers and employees. Nancy noted that while he tried to make it look as though he were in control, it was really Larry who had defused the situation.

Slowly the crowd broke up. Ms. Kussack hurried over to Nancy's side and took her hand comfortingly.

"You poor thing!" she clucked sympathetically. "What an awful ordeal! Come outside and get some fresh air!" Bess, George, and Larry traipsed across the lobby after them.

"I'm okay," Nancy assured Ms. Kussack.

"What happened down there?" Bess demanded. "You look terrible!"

A second voice echoed Bess's. "What's going on here?" It was Alan Charles, and his expression bespoke sheer rage. Not rage at them, Nancy decided, but at the situation in the bank, which was quickly getting out of hand.

"Tear gas, Mr. Charles," Larry answered. "But don't worry. Nobody's badly hurt."

"What about the vault?" Mr. Charles demanded.

Nancy watched as a look of alarm spread slowly across Larry's face. "The vault! The gate's open!"

"Well, let's go down and close it," Mr. Charles said. "And while we're at it, we'll check for damages."

"Uh, Mr. Charles," Larry said softly, "we better wait

53

until the gas clears. I wouldn't want anyone else breathing it in."

"Larry's right," Nancy agreed. "It's not safe now."

"I'll stand guard at the head of the stairs until we can go down," Larry assured Mr. Charles. Without waiting for a response, he hurried back across the lobby. After a few minutes he motioned to Mr. Charles and Nancy, and they joined him. "It should be okay by now," he said. "I'll go down first. Don't anybody come after me until I give the signal."

Nancy and the others waited at the top of the stairs, watching closely as he made his way down to the basement. He waved his guard's hat in front of his face to clear the air. Then he rounded the curve in the stairs and disappeared.

A moment later he came back into view. "It's okay," he called up to them. "It doesn't smell too good, but there's no danger."

Mr. Charles was down the stairs in an instant, with Nancy after him. As they rounded the last curve of the stairs, a faint hint of tear gas still hung in the air and remnants of the metal grenade lay scattered all over the floor. Other than that, the vault area looked exactly as it had earlier.

Larry and Mr. Charles unlocked the second gate and stepped into the steel vault while Nancy stooped to study the metal shards that had once been the grenade. She searched for identifying marks, but there were none. Disappointed, she rose to her feet. Someone at the bank had to know she was investigating. And whoever it was wanted desperately to get her off the case—either by killing her, as the car incident showed, or by scaring her with the grenade. But there was no way of knowing who was responsible—at least not yet.

54

Larry emerged from the vault. "Clean as a whistle inside," he informed her. "All we really need is a broom and some fans to clear the air."

Mr. Charles popped his head out. "Larry's right," he confirmed. "I'll have the janitor do a good clean-up tonight." Mr. Charles checked his watch. "It's already after five o'clock. Time to lock up." He glanced around. "Where's Maurice?" he asked irritably. "He should have been down here by now to enter the alarm code."

Larry shrugged. "He's always a few minutes late."

Mr. Charles sighed in exasperation. "Grun has been nothing but trouble all day," he said. "I'll go see if I can find him. And while I'm at it, I'll get the janitor." He sprinted up the stairs, and Larry closed the outer gate behind him.

The guard smiled at Nancy. "Back in two shakes," he said. He paused behind his desk and picked up a maroon nylon duffel bag. Then, stepping through the inside gate, he headed for the vault. Nancy watched him make his final inspection for the night. First, he walked through the vault and opened the door to each of the three cubicles inside. Then he entered one of them and shut the door.

A few minutes later he emerged wearing tan slacks, a clean white shirt, and black suspenders. "That's my dressing room," he informed Nancy, smiling. Placing his duffel bag on the floor, he pushed the heavy door. It swung easily and noiselessly shut.

In another instant Maurice came rushing down the stairs. He wheezed, slightly out of breath. Nancy noticed tiny droplets of perspiration on his balding forehead. Mr. Charles chased after him, a few steps behind.

"I'm sorry I'm late," he was saying to his boss, "but I

55

was on the phone with a customer." He paused while Larry opened the outer gate. As he entered the vestibule and caught sight of the exploded grenade, his eyes opened wide. "Wow, what a mess!" he exclaimed. "I didn't expect it to be so bad!"

Nancy studied Maurice's face. What had he meant by that last comment? That he hadn't expected such a mess when he planned the attack? Or that he'd heard the explosion and figured it couldn't be all that bad?

"Never mind that now," Mr. Charles said, frowning. "It's your job to enter the code and you're late. There's no excuse for that."

Maurice nibbled at his lips nervously, but he didn't say another word. Instead, he hurried over to where Larry was standing just inside the open inner gate. Mr. Charles gave a nod, and Larry began to turn the metal wheel on the outside of the door, first one direction, then the other, then the first way again. Meanwhile, Maurice pressed a series of numbers into the electronic alarm panel. Nancy watched his movements carefully, until a noise at the top of the stairs distracted her. For an instant she feared a second grenade. Then a slender old man swung around the curve of the stairs, a bucket, mop, and broom grasped in his hands.

"Whew!" the janitor exclaimed. "Mr. Charles, I can mop up the floor, but I don't think I can do anything about the smell."

Nancy turned her attention back to the vault. Larry and Maurice had finished securing it for the night, and now Larry grasped the inside gate, to push it shut. Mr. Charles stopped him with a hand on his sleeve. "You'd better leave that open. Don will have to clean in there too. I'll stay down here and lock the gates once this mess has been taken care of." Mr. Charles beckoned the janitor over, and the man began his work.

"Well, then, I'll say goodbye for the evening," Larry said, waving his hand.

"Me too," Nancy said. "See you tomorrow."

Secretly she couldn't help wondering why Mr. Charles insisted on leaving the gate open. Was there something about the bank president she was missing? Like a criminal tendency?

"Goodbye, Nancy, Larry," Mr. Charles called as they headed up the stairs.

Back up in the lobby, Bess and George were waiting with similar worried frowns, but their expressions lifted as they saw Nancy reappear. "Glad you're back," George said. "You know, we're really nervous after everything that's happened."

"I'm so happy this day is over." Bess sighed. "Let's get out of here." She swung her bag over her shoulder and started eagerly for the door.

"Hold on a sec," Nancy said, stopping them. "Can you guys wait a couple more minutes? There's just one last thing I need to check out before we go."

"But everyone's gone home," Bess moaned. She bit her finger nervously.

It was true. The lobby was empty of customers. Only a few bank employees remained, and all of them were wrapping up their last business and heading for the door.

"It's Ms. Sobel," Nancy explained. "She's been visiting the vault practically every morning and evening. I want to know what she's up to. If she's still here, I'm going to go see her. Maybe I can pick up a clue."

"Let's wait outside," Bess suggested as the guard on duty motioned that he wanted to lock the big front doors.

"I'll be only five minutes," Nancy promised, then sprinted for the stairs and took them two at a time.

Halfway down the long, dim hallway, she spotted a brass nameplate marked Assistant Branch Manager. The office door stood slightly ajar. Pausing just before she reached the portal, Nancy peered in through the tiny crack. If she could catch Ms. Sobel off guard, she might be able to learn something.

The older woman sat behind her desk, her steady gaze trained on the screen of her personal computer. She seemed totally absorbed in her work, smiling slightly to herself and pausing only occasionally to take a sip from a can of soda. Bracing herself for yet another rude conversation, Nancy knocked loudly on the door.

"Come in," Ms. Sobel called.

Nancy opened the door wide. She noticed that a scowl slid onto Ms. Sobel's face the moment the assistant branch manager saw her.

Nancy walked quickly over to the desk, hoping to catch a glimpse of what was on the computer screen that had made Ms. Sobel smile so. But Ms. Sobel was too fast for her. By the time Nancy got close enough to see, she'd tapped a key and the screen had gone blank.

"I'm sorry to interrupt you—" Nancy began.

"Then don't," the assistant manager snapped. "Can't you see I'm busy?"

Nancy forced herself not to react. She was determined not to let Ms. Sobel's rudeness get to her. "I know you're busy," she said calmly, "but there's something I wanted to say. It seems like we got off on the wrong foot earlier. I thought maybe we could try to start out all over again and this time do it right."

"Why, that's a fine idea." Ms. Sobel smiled, but there was no warmth in her eyes. "The first rule is, interns do not interrupt branch managers for no reason. Learn that one, *very* well."

The nasty words felt like a slap. Nancy wasn't sure how to respond, and for a moment she just stared at Ms. Sobel, stunned by the woman's rudeness.

Ms. Sobel half rose and leaned forward over her desk. "I believe I made myself clear." She pointed to the door. "You can go out the same way you came in."

"Pardon me," said Nancy coolly. Without saying goodbye, she turned and left the room.

"I can't believe she was so nasty!" Bess exclaimed. She pushed back her half-finished plate of goulash— her second helping—and gazed from Nancy to George to Nancy's father, to the Drews' housekeeper, Hannah Gruen. Nancy had invited her friends over for dinner. It was the least she could do for them after the day's hair-raising events. Hannah had treated them all to a specially cooked meal, and they'd all relaxed a bit while Nancy filled her family in on the details of the case.

"Well, what do you think about events at the bank, Hannah?" Bess asked.

Hannah Gruen had raised Nancy almost like a daughter after Nancy's mother had died years before. All the girls came to her for her caring advice. Still, Nancy wished Bess hadn't asked her for it just now. She knew what was coming.

"What I think," Hannah said in no uncertain terms, "is that Nancy should get off this case before she really gets hurt!" She shook her head for emphasis, but her gentle eyes showed fear more than anything else.

"It's not as serious as that," Nancy said calmly. "I think someone's just trying to scare me, that's all. If they'd wanted to kill me, they'd have used a real grenade, not one filled with tear gas." Secretly, she agreed with Hannah—at least with the first part of what she'd said—but she didn't want either the housekeeper or her father to worry.

"Do you think Ms. Sobel could have been the one who threw the smoke bomb?" Nancy's father suggested. Lean and handsome, Carson Drew sat at the head of the table, looking every bit as worried about his daughter as Hannah did. "It sounds to me like she was conspicuously absent when you and the guard came up from the basement."

"Yeah," George agreed. "Maybe she was hiding out in her office afterward, trying to look busy. That would explain why she was so angry when you confronted her. Maybe she felt guilty."

"It's entirely possible," Nancy said. "But we have no way of knowing unless we can prove she was near the stairs right before the explosion." She looked back and forth between Bess and George. "Are you *sure* you didn't see anything?" she asked them.

"We were in the back," George said. "We didn't know what was going on until we heard that big bang."

Crash! Bess's voice was drowned out by what seemed like an echo of the afternoon's explosion. In the next instant the group was bathed in a shower of glass as the dining room window shattered into a million sharp pieces. Nancy whirled around. A large rock lay on the Drews' carpet. A piece of white paper was wrapped around the rock, and a rubber band held it in place.

Nancy could feel her temper rising. Someone had purposely thrown that rock through their window! She had to know what the note said, but more important, who had thrown it. She dashed to the front door, banging it open and rushing outside. The others

60

weren't far behind her. She peered down the street just as a white convertible sports car with prominent fins on the back went screeching around the corner. Before it disappeared from view, Nancy made out two figures in the front seat. One of them had curly pale-colored hair that flew wildly in the wind. As the car took off, one of the people whooped loudly with cruel laughter. Still, Nancy couldn't get a good glimpse of either one.

Disappointed, Nancy trooped inside with the others. Well, maybe the note would hold some clues. Reaching past the broken glass, she picked up the rock. She pulled on the rubber band so hard that it broke. Then she unfolded the note.

"What does it say?" asked Bess breathlessly.

Slowly Nancy read out loud. " 'Stay away from the vault, or we'll put *you* in cold storage. You can bank on it!' "

8

Intruder in the Night

"They couldn't make it any plainer than that," Hannah burst out, pointing emphatically at the note. "Nancy, they mean to *kill* you."

"It's just a threat," Nancy hastened to say. "They wouldn't really do it." But she didn't believe her own words, and she knew she couldn't fool Hannah either. "I didn't get a good look at the people in the car," she added, quickly changing the subject. "Odd car, though. Some sort of old-make convertible from the fifties."

"Nineteen fifty-seven, to be exact," Nancy's father informed her.

The girls and Hannah turned to him, amazed. "How did you know that?" Bess demanded, letting out a laugh. "I never figured you for an old-car buff."

"I'm not," Carson Drew agreed, smiling. "But the 1957 Ford Skyliner is a real classic. Back when I was in high school, it was *the* car to have. I must have spent hours poring over car magazines, taking in its every detail. But the Skyliner was a rare car—they only made a few thousand of them—so I never got to drive one."

Nancy feigned shock. "Dad! And I thought all you ever studied were your schoolbooks!"

"Those too," Carson said, shaking his head ruefully.

"I wish the drivers' faces were as recognizable as their car," Nancy said, disappointed. "Too bad they didn't come closer."

"I'm glad they didn't," Hannah said. "Breaking that window was close enough."

"I agree," said Nancy's father, his light tone changing to one of utmost seriousness. "They've already tried to hurt you twice, and this incident proves they know where we live. Next time, I don't think they'll stop with rock throwing."

Hannah shuddered. "Nancy, I'm worried."

"Maybe you should let the police know what's going on," Carson continued. "I think this case is getting too dangerous for you to handle alone."

Nancy frowned, then shook her head. "First of all," she told her father, "I'm not alone." She wrapped her arms around Bess's and George's shoulders. "I've got great assistance from my two best buddies. Second," Nancy continued, "I gave my word to Mr. Charles that we'd keep the investigation confidential. Third, if anyone else gets involved, we might scare the criminals away, and then we'll never catch them."

Nancy studied her father's face. He was wearing his "I'm not convinced" look. "Okay," she said, offering a compromise, "how about this. If anything else happens, I *will* go to the police."

Carson Drew pressed his lips together and threw his

hands up in the air. "I should know better than to argue with you." He sighed. "Just promise me one thing."

"Sure, Dad," Nancy agreed. "What is it?"

River Heights' number-one lawyer looked anxiously into his daughter's eyes. "Please—solve this case fast!"

The next morning Nancy smoothed her red dress and straightened her black blazer as she, George, and Bess strode up the marble steps of the Bentley Bank. She figured they'd already been seen so often together that it didn't matter if they arrived as a group. Maybe people would think they'd just gotten friendly on the job. In any case, from now on the girls would be working as a team.

The security guard at the top of the stairs unlocked the front door to let them in, then locked it again once they'd stepped inside. Nancy checked her watch. "We have a couple of minutes before we have to be at our 'jobs,'" she said. "Let's go downstairs and check on Larry, see if he's okay after yesterday's ordeal. Besides, it might be a good idea to check on the vault too."

"Good thinking," George agreed, heading across the lobby. "Around here, you can't tell *what* might have happened since yesterday."

As they made their way downstairs, Nancy thought of the previous day's grenade. Anyone could have stood at the top of the flight, pitched the smoke bomb down, and let gravity do the rest. As they reached the bottom, Nancy was glad to see Mr. Charles standing by Larry's desk. She needed to talk to him. Larry, still in his street clothes, was unlocking the gate that led to the vault.

Mr. Charles turned to greet them with a smile. His nervous mood of the day before seemed to have vanished with a good night's rest. "I'll unlock the outer gate for you in a moment," he said. He and Larry entered the vault area. The girls watched from behind the closed gate while the two men went through their daily ritual of unlocking the vault and disarming the alarm. When they were done, Larry pulled on the door and it glided noiselessly outward.

"Gotta make my quick change into the uniform now." Larry grinned and headed inside the vault with his duffel bag.

He hadn't gone more than a couple of steps when Nancy's eyes gazed across the sparkling floor of the vault. But the floor wasn't completely clear. A glittering object lay near the wall, small and round, like a ball. It was too even a shape to be a piece of the grenade. "What's that?" she asked.

Larry stopped abruptly and gazed around the vault. "Well, I'll be—" He gasped in disbelief.

Nancy watched Mr. Charles steel himself for more bad news. "Now what?" he asked. Taking a few steps forward, he bent down to pick up the object. For several seconds he studied it. He glanced, worried, at Nancy. Then he said to Larry, his voice low, "How about checking the tape." Clearly, he wanted to make this discovery without an outside witness.

Larry seemed to understand. "I'll need my tool chest to crack that camera open," he said. "I'll be right back."

Larry opened the outer gate and ushered the three girls into the vestibule. "You'll be okay in here with Mr. Charles." He pointed to the notebook on his desk. "Don't forget to sign in." Then he disappeared up the steps.

Quickly, the girls followed his instructions. Then Nancy looked at the object in Mr. Charles's hand. "May I see that?" she asked.

65

Pressing his lips together in silent frustration. Mr. Charles dropped the ball into Nancy's palm. It was a clip-on earring, round and encrusted with dark green gems. For its size, it was very heavy. "It looks old-fashioned," Nancy said, rolling the earring around on her hand.

Then Nancy noticed something else. Caught in the clip on the back of the earring were several strands of gray hair. She couldn't help wondering if the hair belonged to Evelyn Sobel. Perhaps while going through drawers of expensive jewelry in the vault the night before, she'd been tempted to try one on and—

Nancy's thoughts were interrupted as Larry reentered the vault, a stepladder in one hand and a toolbox in the other. He flipped the box open, grabbed a screwdriver, then set up the ladder and climbed up to the video camera. Soon he had pried open the camera's metal casing. Slipping out the cassette, he handed it to Mr. Charles.

"I'm going upstairs to play the tape," Mr. Charles said. "Perhaps you girls should come upstairs too. It's after nine—time for all of us to get to work." He motioned with his head, and Nancy knew his words were just to protect their cover. He wanted them to see the tape.

Moments later the four sat perplexed before the president's VCR. They had fast-forwarded the entire tape and seen nothing but static.

"Erased!" Mr. Charles exclaimed, slamming his fist down on the top of his desk. "How could they erase the tape and rob the vault at the same time?"

"They couldn't," Nancy said simply. "But maybe they *replaced* the tape with one of their own." She turned the earring over and over absently in her hand.

66

"As for robbery, maybe they've taken jewelry, maybe not. Until one of your box holders reports something missing, we won't know."

"But if there still isn't anything gone, what are they looking for?" Bess asked, frustration flushing her cheeks.

Nancy shook her head. "I have no idea. If we could answer that question, it might help us figure out who's involved. Mr. Charles, what *do* people store in their boxes?"

"I'm afraid I can't tell you that," Mr. Charles said, "because I don't know myself. We don't have any idea what our box holders put in the vault. It's the customer's right to privacy."

"You mean they can put anything they want in there?" Bess asked.

"Anything," Mr. Charles said, nodding.

"Even things that are illegal?" Bess insisted, incredulous.

"They're not supposed to," Mr. Charles told the girls. "When they sign for their box, they agree not to use it for anything improper. Unfortunately, we have no way of knowing whether our customers stick to that agreement."

Slowly, an idea was forming in Nancy's mind. Bess had stumbled on a brilliant explanation. Maybe the thieves hadn't stolen jewels because they'd be too easy to trace. The owner of the gems would call the police, and then it might quickly be all over for the crooks. But if the criminals took something illegal—something that wasn't supposed to be in a box at all—then the theft would never get reported, there'd be no investigation, and they'd go scot-free!

"Mr. Charles," Nancy said seriously, "do you have a complete list of all the box holders?"

"Of course," Mr. Charles said. "We keep an updated list on our computer."

"Could we take a look at it? It might give us some ideas about what's being kept in the vault and what the thieves are after."

Mr. Charles pressed his lips together. "That list is confidential," he said, "and accessible by a secret code word that only I have."

Nancy didn't try to persuade him. She knew Mr. Charles would have to come to his own decision.

"It *would* be a breach of banking procedure," Mr. Charles went on slowly. "But on the other hand, I'm the one who sets procedure, so I guess I can break it in this situation. I'll bring up the list of customers and cross-reference it with payment schedules and vault visits. You can study the information and see if it's helpful."

"Maybe George can take care of that," Nancy suggested, glancing at her friend.

"Sure," George agreed. "I can come up and do it on my lunch break. Maurice already oriented me on the computer downstairs. Are all the bank's computers the same?"

"Yes," said Mr. Charles. "In fact, they share a central memory."

"So whatever is entered into one is accessible from any other?" George asked.

"Exactly," said Mr. Charles. "To get into the system, you need a password. Most bank employees know it. And there are certain classified files—like the vault safe-depositor list—that you need a second password to get into. I'll set you up with everything you need at lunch."

"Great," George said. "Well, I guess we'd better get to work before people start wondering where we are."

Mr. Charles opened his office door, and the girls filed into Ms. Kussack's area. The secretary was spooning coffee grounds into the coffeemaker.

"Good morning," she called as the girls stepped past, then went back to the coffeemaker.

As the three girls began their trek down the long hallway, Nancy thanked George for giving up her lunch hour to pore over the computer lists.

"Oh, don't mention it. It'll be fun." George paused a moment. "I always wanted to be a computer geek," she joked.

After all the activity of the day before, the morning was a bit of a letdown. Banking business as usual could be pretty boring, Nancy realized. So it was with a twinge of excitement that, just before noon, Nancy spotted a familiar slim figure entering the bank's front door. Jill Adler shook her black hair, seemed determined as she headed for the tellers' windows.

"Jill!" Nancy called, hurrying to her.

Jill Adler turned, recognized Nancy, and smiled. "Hi!"

"What are you doing here?" Nancy asked. "Are you going to ask for your job back?"

"No," answered Jill. "But I have good news! Last night Maurice called me and said he'd changed his mind. He broke it off with his new girlfriend and wants to get back together with me."

"So what are you going to do?" Nancy wanted to know.

"I'm not sure," Jill said. "I still think he acted pretty badly, and I don't really know if things can ever be the same between us. But I have to see him, that much I *do* know."

69

Nancy pursed her lips. She found Maurice's behavior suspicious.

"Besides," Jill said, "I'm dying of curiosity. Maurice said he wants to give me something—something sparkly!" she continued happily. "We're having lunch at Kathy's Café. And Nancy, he said it's *not* just a ring!"

Nancy sucked in her breath. She had to admit that *she* was curious too. Just where was a bank teller getting the money for all this jewelry?

"Oh, there's Maurice now." Jill pointed as the head teller stepped from behind the Plexiglas. "Wish me luck," she murmured. With a quick wave, she ran to him. Just as quickly, Nancy ran to find Bess.

"I've got good news for you," Nancy said, stepping up to her friend's teller window.

"You won the lottery and you want to deposit a million dollars in our bank?" Bess teased.

"No." Nancy laughed. "It's time for lunch, and I'm treating you to a meal at Kathy's Café."

Nancy held the Kathy's Café menu in front of her face for the second time in two days. But her gaze wasn't on the lists of burgers and salads. Instead, her eyes wandered to the cozy couple sitting two tables away. She'd picked her spot carefully, just for the view. Maurice and Jill had pulled their chairs close to each other. Maurice had his arm around Jill, and she nestled against him.

In a moment the waiter came over and took Nancy and Bess's order.

"If I were her, I wouldn't trust him again so fast," Bess commented, nodding toward Jill. "I mean, think about it. He dumps her yesterday morning, but he wants her back the same night? It doesn't make sense."

"That's exactly what I was thinking," Nancy said. "And I can't explain it. But if Maurice gives her what I think he's going to, we may have some evidence against them."

The waiter returned with a burger for Bess, a steaming bowl of soup for Nancy, and two shakes. The girls were just digging in when Maurice unwrapped his arm from around Jill's shoulders and reached into his jacket pocket.

"This is it, this is it!" Nancy whispered excitedly to Bess.

The two friends watched as he pulled out a long, thin black velvet box and, whispering in Jill's ear, handed it to her. She flashed a twenty-four-carat smile as she flipped the lid. Even from two tables away it was hard to miss the glare of light reflecting off diamonds and emeralds.

"A bracelet!" Jill cried, sounding thrilled. "Maurice, you shouldn't have done it!"

Maurice leaned back in his chair, looking one hundred percent confident. "Don't worry," he said smugly. "You ought to know by now, there's plenty more where that came from."

9

New Suspicions

Bess gasped and her eyes grew round. "Did you hear that?" she whispered. "He might just as well have said, 'Don't worry, I stole the bracelet out of the vault!' Maurice and Jill *must* be working together."

"Not so fast, Bess," Nancy cautioned. "I agree this looks like another piece of evidence, but it's still not conclusive."

"What more do you need?" Bess asked, exasperated. "Maurice knows half the vault code, and he's got a lot of expensive jewelry he can't afford. All we have to do now is prove he drives a white 'fifty-seven Skyliner, and we've got him nailed!" With an air of finality, Bess chomped down on her Kathyburger, which was topped with mushrooms and three kinds of cheese.

Nancy's spoon stirred endless circles in her chicken noodle soup. "It's not that I disagree with you, Bess," she said quietly to her friend. "Some of the facts do point to Maurice. But we have no proof. And what's more, he might be involved, yet that doesn't necessarily mean Jill's working with him. She's so nice—and vulnerable. She just doesn't strike me as the criminal type."

"Well, what about Evelyn Sobel?" Bess suggested. "There's a lot of evidence pointing to her—her strange behavior, her visits to the vault, and the fact that she knows the combination. Put her and Maurice together, and that vault just pops open!" Pleased with herself, Bess took a long sip of chocolate milk shake through a plastic straw.

"It does add up," Nancy agreed, staring at her spoon as it swirled through the noodles.

"Not to mention the leather glove," Bess added.

Nancy looked up, staring intently at her friend. "That's where the Sobel theory falls flat," she said firmly.

"What do you mean?" asked Bess. "The glove is the most obvious link to Ms. Sobel."

"That's the problem," said Nancy. "It's *too* obvious. Think about it. If Ms. Sobel was the one who broke into Mr. Charles's safe, she might have worn gloves to avoid leaving fingerprints. But why would she take one off? She'd never do that until she was safely outside his office."

Bess punched at her chocolate shake with her straw. "I never thought of that," she admitted.

"Which means it's more likely that someone else left the glove there," Nancy concluded.

"You mean someone's setting Ms. Sobel up?" asked Bess.

"It's possible," Nancy said, finally digging into her soup. "In which case, Maurice would have to be working with someone else. Maybe with Larry Jaye.

Larry knows the vault combination, and Maurice knows the alarm code. Together the two of them could get into the vault."

Bess looked up from her food, surprised. "How could it be Larry?" she asked. "You know he didn't throw the tear gas yesterday, because he was with you when it happened. Besides, he seems pretty nice too."

"Maurice might have thrown it," Nancy said. "Larry could have just played along."

"Well, what about the break-in to Mr. Charles's safe?" Bess asked. "You said Larry was with you when that happened too."

"He looks innocent so far," Nancy agreed. "I'm just saying we can't rule him out."

Nancy and Bess had almost finished their meal when Maurice and Jill rose from their table, arm in arm. It looked as though the two *would* reconcile. Nancy wasn't sure whether to be happy or not. As they approached, Nancy noticed the diamond and emerald bracelet sparkling on Jill's wrist. She smiled, expecting Jill to stop and show off her gift, but Jill walked right past. Puzzled, Nancy stared after the couple as they stepped onto the sidewalk.

"Nice and vulnerable, huh?" Bess said. "First she acts like your friend, then she ignores you. She doesn't seem too nice to me."

Nancy shrugged and pulled her wallet out of her purse. "At this point, we can't rule *anyone* out." She left some money on the table. "We'd better get back. I wonder if George has found anything useful in the computer."

A few minutes later the girls were back at the Bentley Bank, peering over George's shoulder at a computer printout that she had laid across Alan

Charles's desk. Mr. Charles had pulled up an armchair across from her.

"You won't believe who some of these safe-deposit box holders are," George commented, pointing to a few names on her sheet. "I'm going nuts wondering what's in all of them!" George read a name off her list. "Annette Williams," she explained, "is an elderly widow who is said to keep a safe-deposit box to store her dog's biscuits."

"That was in the computer?" Nancy asked.

"Not exactly," said George. "But there were two names listed for her box, and the second one was Snooky. I asked Mr. Charles, and he said everyone at the bank has heard about her and her dog."

"Of course, it's just rumor," Mr. Charles added.

Nancy laughed. "What else did you find?"

"Well, there's this really rich man, Robert Springett, who's got twenty boxes all to himself. But he's not the big news. In fact, I think I may have discovered the clue we're looking for."

"Don't torture us," said Bess. "Out with it."

"It's about this guy, Bob Davis," George said. "He's been renting a safe-deposit box for years, but he never visits it."

"Maybe he's forgotten he has it," Bess suggested.

"That's not possible," George replied, shaking her head. "You have to pay for the box every year, and Davis has never missed a payment. But it gets more interesting," George continued. "Davis moved away from Bentley over twenty years ago."

"That's odd," Nancy murmured. "Why would he keep a box here if he lives elsewhere?"

"The really important fact is where Mr. Davis moved to," George announced. "You see, Bob Davis moved

75

away because he had to do a little time in the Illinois Federal Penitentiary!"

"Jail?" Nancy exclaimed, her blue eyes lighting up. "I wonder what type of crime he committed. Maybe it's linked to why he'd need a safe-deposit box all these years. If he's been in jail for over twenty years, he must have done something serious. The police would have a record of it."

Mr. Charles thought for a moment. "The *Bentley Times* just ran an article about the local police station's new computer," he said. "Apparently, it's tied in to police stations all over the country. I'm sure you could find out more about Davis there."

"Well, what are we waiting for? Let's get over there," Nancy said.

Mr. Charles gave them easy directions to the police station. "Just do me one favor," he said. "While you're there, don't mention why you're looking for this information. I'd still like to keep this business quiet as long as possible."

"You got it," said Nancy.

"There's just one problem," Bess piped up.

"What's that?" asked Nancy.

"Lunchtime's over," she pointed out. "How can we leave the bank?"

"I'll take care of it," Mr. Charles assured them. "I'll tell Maurice that you're on an errand for me."

"Thanks," said Nancy. "We'll be back before closing time."

A short walk through Bentley's sun-splashed streets brought Nancy, Bess, and George to a two-story cement building. If the rest of Bentley was picturesque, the police station stood out as an eyesore. Even inside, the beige linoleum was worn and the whole place needed a new coat of paint.

At the far end of the room a gray metal desk stood on a low platform. Behind the desk sat a young police officer with short, tightly curled hair and a mustache. A placard sitting on the front of the desk said Sergeant Steven Ramirez.

"Excuse me," said Nancy.

The desk sergeant looked up from his paperwork. "What can I do for you ladies?" he asked.

Nancy had already thought up a cover story. "We're doing a school project on criminals of the twentieth century," she told the sergeant, "and our teacher said you might have information on arrest records."

Sergeant Ramircz's eyes lit up. "You must have heard about our new computer. We're hooked up to police stations all over the country. We've got records on almost every criminal convicted in this country in the past thirty years."

"That's exactly what we're looking for," Nancy said.

"Come around behind the desk," said Sergeant Ramirez, breaking into a grin.

Behind the desk an impressive display had been set up. The technology, Nancy realized, was the very latest. An up-to-the-second black computer monitor rested on a black console. In front of it was a black rod the size of a pencil.

"Where's the keyboard?" George asked.

"Aha!" exclaimed Sergeant Ramirez, pointing one finger up in the air. "Let's find out."

He flipped a switch on the side of the console, and the monitor lit up with a menu of programs. Touching the rod directly to the screen, Ramirez highlighted each item on the menu.

"Oh, I get it," said George. "You don't even need to type. Very advanced."

The sergeant nodded. "Now," he said, "what would you like to know?"

"Well," Nancy began, "we're especially interested in one criminal in particular. His name is Bob Davis."

"Common name," said Ramirez. "Can you tell me anything else about him?"

"He used to live in Bentley," said Nancy. "Now he's in the Illinois Federal Penitentiary."

"That should be enough," Ramirez told her. Touching the rod to the monitor, he called up a second menu, then a third, then a fourth. Finally, the screen came up with text. A mug-shot photograph was perfectly highlighted in the right corner. "His record," Ramirez announced proudly.

Nancy leaned forward eagerly and peered at the screen. At the top, the file said that David Baker was also known as Bob Davis, David Roberts, and Danny Bob Robins. "Are these his aliases?" Nancy asked.

Ramirez glanced at the screen. "Yes. David Baker's his real name."

Baker's list of convictions was long, covering over thirty years of crime. Nancy's eyes ran down the text. Cat burglary, car theft, counterfeiting. But it was only when she got to the final charge that she realized she'd hit pay dirt. Twenty-three years ago, David Baker had been convicted of armed bank robbery!

10

An Unusual Skyline

"Bingo!" cried Bess. "This could be the clue that turns this case around." Realizing she'd said more than she should have in front of the police officer, Bess clamped a hand over her mouth and gave Nancy a guilty look.

Ramirez eyed the girls curiously. "What kind of school project is this, anyway?"

Nancy quickly covered for Bess. "It's sort of like practice detective work," she explained. "Our teacher gave us a case to solve, and our assignment was to find out about Bob Davis. She got his name out of an old Bentley newspaper." Nancy studied the sergeant's face, hoping he wouldn't ask any more questions.

Sergeant Ramirez shrugged, seeming satisfied. "Sounds like fun."

"Baker's got quite a record," Nancy commented, pushing for a few more clues. "Is there any way we can get more information on him?"

"He's got to have a file," Sergeant Ramirez told her. "Let me check." The officer touched the rod to the screen and brought up the main menu again. In less than a minute Nancy found herself staring at a document titled "The Hit and Run Gang."

"The Hit and Run Gang?" Bess asked. "What does that have to do with David Baker?"

"You'll have to read it," said Sergeant Ramirez. "Here, let me print it out for you." He touched the screen again. Instantly, Nancy heard a whirring noise from deep inside the console. Stooping down, Ramirez opened the console door and tore a length of paper out of the printer. Then he separated three pages along the perforations and handed them to Nancy.

"You can read this over there," he told the girls, indicating a row of orange molded plastic chairs along the wall of the lobby.

"Thanks, Sergeant," Nancy said sincerely. "You've been a big help."

The officer flashed a friendly smile. "Hope you get an A," he said with a wink.

Nancy was excited as she and her friends hurried over to the plastic chairs. This was something important. She could feel it. Clearing her throat, she read aloud from the computer printout.

"David Baker, a former employee of the U.S. Mint, was convicted of stealing government plates and counterfeiting ten-dollar bills. He escaped from prison and later became a member of the notorious 'Hit and Run Gang,' a highly successful team of bank robbers.

"The Hit and Run Gang, headed by the husband-and-wife team of Jake and Jasmine Sims, robbed over one hundred banks. In their final robbery, in which they got away with over half a million dollars from the Rushton Savings Bank in

Rushton, Ohio, most of the gang members were captured. Only Jasmine, Jake, and Baker escaped. All three disappeared. The money was never recovered.

"Baker moved to Bentley, Illinois, where he lived under the alias Bob Davis. He was finally arrested by federal investigators at his home there. He is currently serving a life sentence in the Illinois Federal Penitentiary. Jake and Jasmine Sims remain at large."

"Wow." George let out a low whistle and shook her head. "That's quite a story. Maybe it's that half a million dollars that Baker has hidden inside his safe-deposit box."

"Maybe," Nancy said. "That would explain why someone is working so hard to find Baker's box."

"*And* why they haven't risked stealing anything else from the vault," George added. "If they get the half a million, Baker can't even report it missing, since he's not supposed to have it in the first place. Besides, he's not even around to open the box and see that it's gone."

"Wait a second, you guys," Bess said slowly. She was staring at the floor, her brow wrinkled in concentration. "I think I've heard of Jake and Jasmine Sims before. And also of the Hit and Run Gang. But I can't quite pin down what."

"How did you hear about them?" Nancy asked. "Sometimes that can help you remember a story."

The crease in Bess's brow intensified. Then suddenly her face brightened and she snapped her fingers. "Of course! It was in that funny old movie. They made a film about those two a long time ago—like, twenty years ago. I think it was called *Jake and Jasmine.*"

"What does a movie have to do with this case?"

81

George asked, sounding annoyed. "It's not going to have a scene where Baker walks into the vault of the Bentley Bank and deposits . . . whatever he deposits."

"No," said Nancy, "but it might give us some information we don't know yet."

"We could rent the movie," Bess suggested. "Maybe it's on video."

"Great idea, Bess," Nancy said. She slid out of the chair and stepped back to Sergeant Ramirez's desk. He was hunched forward, reading a report. "Thanks for your help, Sergeant," she said.

Sergeant Ramirez looked up and smiled. "Don't mention it," he said.

Nancy smiled back. "Do you happen to know where there's a video store nearby?" she asked.

Sergeant Ramirez nodded. "Vera's World of Video. It's right down the street, across from the hospital."

"Thanks," said Nancy. With a quick wave the three girls left the station.

As they strolled through the summer afternoon sun, Nancy decided the day was turning out just perfectly. It felt as though they were making some real progress with the case. Just past Bentley Municipal Park a dark-haired girl with a huge smile came into sight.

Jill Adler! Nancy realized with a start. Even from fifty feet away Nancy could see Jill's new bracelet sparkling in the sunlight.

"Listen," Nancy said to her friends, thinking quickly, "I need to talk with Jill. Alone. Maybe you could catch some rays in that little park over there. Jill's got some explaining to do."

"No problem," George said. She grabbed Bess, who seemed to be hypnotized by the sight of Jill's bracelet. As the two cousins crossed the street, Nancy slowed her pace. She still found it hard to believe Jill had ignored her at Kathy's Café. It just didn't fit with the girl's previous friendliness. Nancy decided to say nothing, to see if Jill would ignore her again.

But now the old Jill was back. "Nancy!" she called, waving the arm with the bracelet. "I'm so glad I ran into you! Notice anything different about me?" She held out the emerald-and-diamond piece of jewelry for Nancy to see.

"It's beautiful," Nancy acknowledged. Indeed, it was one of the most stunning—and expensive—pieces Nancy had ever laid eyes on.

"Maurice gave it to me at lunch," Jill said, smiling.

"I know," Nancy told her. Taking a deep breath, she decided to confront Jill directly. "I was sitting two tables away from you, and you walked right by me."

Jill's expression twisted instantly into an apologetic frown. "Oh, Nancy," she cried anxiously. "I'm so sorry. I didn't even see you! I was so excited about my gift—and getting back together with Maurice. I—I guess I didn't notice anything else."

Jill certainly seemed sincere, but Nancy couldn't tell for sure. Still, she did basically like Jill. And anyway, the other woman was more likely to open up if she acted friendly. "I guess that's why they say love is blind."

Jill gave Nancy's arm a squeeze. "Thank you for being so understanding," she said. "I knew I liked you as soon as I met you. It's so strange. I've only known you a day, but somehow I feel I know so much about you."

Nancy studied Jill's face closely to see if there was another meaning behind Jill's statement. Did she mean she knew the real reason she, Nancy, was in Bentley?

Was there a hidden warning in her words? Her expression was friendly, but her tone held just a tinge of something cooler.

Nancy nodded to Jill. "I'll remember that. Anyway, I'm late for work, so I'd better go."

Jill smiled. "I know that feeling—rushing back before your superior notices you've been gone an hour and a half for lunch." She laughed. "I'm sure I'll see you very soon," she added. "'Bye."

Again Nancy wondered if something lay hidden in Jill's words. But the other woman was already setting off down the street. When Jill was out of sight, Nancy motioned to Bess and George to rejoin her.

"Well?" Bess asked as the three of them continued down the hill toward the video store. "Did she explain why she acted rude?"

"She says she was so excited she didn't notice me," Nancy said. "I wanted to believe her, but I just wasn't convinced one hundred percent. Anyway, we'd better get to Vera's World of Video. We've been out of the bank too long as it is."

Bentley Hospital was just down the block. Nancy could see its two redbrick towers high above the other roofs. Across from its elegant curving driveway, a flashing neon sign announced: Vera's World of Video—a Thousand Films to Choose From. "This is it," Nancy said, crossing to the store. A bell jingled as they opened the door to enter.

The video store was dark and musty. Rows of shelves, floor to ceiling, held jumbled stacks of black plastic video cassette cases. Behind the counter, mounted close to the ceiling, a video monitor was playing a recently released movie. The scene showed hundreds of teenagers running out of a movie theater, pursued by a giant pair of high-top sneakers. The sneakers

84

stomped menacingly behind them, threatening to crush them all.

A plump, middle-aged woman with heavy eye make-up and a voluminous, loose-fitting dress stood behind the counter. "I'm Vera," she announced. "If it's on video, I've got it. What can I do for you?"

Bess leaned forward over the counter. "I think there was a movie made about twenty years ago called *Jake and Jasmine* or *Jasmine and Jake.* It was about a romantic pair of bank robbers. Do you have it?"

"Of course I've got it!" Vera said indignantly. "I just have to find it. Oh, by the way, you got it right the first time. *Jake and Jasmine* it is."

Vera rummaged around in the shelves behind her, muttering softly to herself. Her movements jostled the tapes and several cassettes fell around her feet. But Vera didn't seem to notice or to care. She merely kept searching through the cluttered stacks. After several moments she triumphantly held a cassette up and handed it to Bess. Nancy and George crowded around to get a closer look.

Under the title *Jake and Jasmine* was a picture of an attractive couple staring into each other's eyes. The woman was so young, no more than about twenty, with dark curly hair. She wore an expensive-looking sweater set and pearls. The young man, also around twenty, had straight black hair that fell over one eye. He wore a ripped shirt and overalls.

Bess turned the cassette over and read the ad blurb aloud: "'She came from the wealthiest family in Piskatchitee, Iowa. He came from the wrong side of the tracks. She had everything money could buy—except excitement. He gave her more than she bargained for. True love takes a ride on the wild side.'"

"This is a romance," George complained. "I know

85

they're criminals and all, but it's like Romeo and Juliet. How's that going to help us?"

"We won't know till we check it out," Nancy said. "I just wish we didn't have to wait until we get home to see it." As if mocking her, the giant sneakers on the video monitor let out a horrible laugh. She glanced up at the screen. Hmm, maybe they *didn't* have to wait. "Uh, excuse me, but could we preview this movie?" she asked Vera.

Vera looked at the girls suspiciously. "Do you really want to rent it?" she asked. "Or are you just trying to get a freebie?"

"Of course we want to rent it," Nancy assured her. "But first we want to get a taste of it to make sure it's worth seeing."

Vera sighed again. She turned off the sneaker movie just as the giant sneakers were tying up a man with their shoelaces. The VCR spit out the old cassette, and Vera popped in *Jake and Jasmine.*

"You can see the first five minutes," she said, waving a finger at them. "After that, you either rent it or fly."

Vera pressed the play button. The girls turned attentively to watch the screen as the credits rolled over a scene of a small-town high school. A harmonica crooned mournfully in the background.

The credits stopped rolling, and the young female star of the movie strolled out the front door of the high school, her long dark hair swinging innocently around her face. She was expensively dressed in a cashmere sweater and a string of pearls.

Nancy stood engrossed, searching for a clue. Jasmine's friends—the classy set at school—kept complaining about how Jasmine's father was too strict. "He never lets you go out," one of the girls whined. "All

86

you ever do is stay home and study. It's *boring*, Jasmine, *boring*."

Jasmine let out a huge sigh. "It's true," she wailed. "Sometimes I feel like a prisoner in my own house! I wish there were some way to break free, but"—she wiped away a tear—"I don't dare disobey him."

For a moment Jasmine's friends tried to comfort her. Then came the roar of a car engine. Jasmine and her friends jumped back as the black-haired male lead pulled his car off the main road. He cut across the school lawn, heading straight for them. He was shouting like a wild man—and driving a 1957 white Ford Skyliner!

11

All Locked Up

Still staring at the TV screen, Nancy clutched her friends' arms. The car Jake was driving in the movie was exactly the same kind of car that had raced past her house the night before. It was all the same—the car, the wild yells, even Jasmine's curly hair. Could the two people in the car the previous night have been Jake and Jasmine?

But the bank robbers would be her dad's age now, Nancy calculated. Would they really go joy riding in a car straight out of the 1950s at their age? And why come out of hiding to do it—why be so conspicuous after so many years? Most of all, could Jake and Jasmine possibly hide their past so well that they'd be able to get jobs at the bank? But even if they *were* the ones breaking into the vault, Nancy still didn't know what they were after. It was a real puzzle.

Still, she tried to think things through logically. If Jake and Jasmine were making a comeback, it ruled out two suspects: Maurice and Jill. They were both too young. Then who *was* old enough? Nancy ran through the possibilities in her mind. Larry Jaye? Evelyn Sobel? Or maybe it was some other older bank employee she hadn't even considered yet.

Nancy sighed. This clue had made things even more confusing than they'd been before!

"It's *got* to be them," Bess said as if reading Nancy's thoughts. "I may not know a lot about cars, but I'd recognize that one anywhere."

"Well, the car *is* the same," Nancy agreed, "but we'd better not jump to conclusions. I mean, that car might just be a movie prop! Jake and Jasmine might never have even owned a Skyliner in real life."

"Come on, Nancy. It's more than a coincidence," George told her, "and you know it. Your dad said the Skyliner was rare even in 1957, that they made only a couple thousand of them. Now two of them show up in two days! Admit it—something is going on here."

Vera had been impatiently tapping her fingers on the counter as the three girls talked. "I'm sure this is a very fascinating conversation," she cut in, "but I don't have time to stand around all day listening to you argue about cars. Do you want to rent the movie or not?" With one swift movement she switched off the VCR, then stood staring at them with her hands on her wide hips.

Nancy pulled her wallet out of her purse, then handed Vera some money and her credit card. Vera wrote down the number on a slip, then took the money. "It's got to be back before five tomorrow, or there's a late fee."

"It won't be late," promised Bess. "We'll return it first thing tomorrow morning." She picked up the cassette, and the girls turned to go.

As they stepped onto the pavement, Nancy turned to

Bess and George with a conspiratorial smile on her face. "I'm not so sure this movie *isn't* going to be late," she told them.

"Stop being cryptic," Bess said, "and tell us what's up."

"Call your folks and tell them you won't be home tonight," said Nancy. "We're spending the night inside the vault."

"What?" Bess shrieked.

"Nancy, you've got to be kidding!" George chimed in.

"Dead serious," Nancy insisted. "Whoever these criminals are, they still haven't found what they're looking for, otherwise they wouldn't still be hanging around the bank. Now that they know we're on their tail, they must be getting desperate. That means they'll have to act fast. So there's a good chance they'll try another break-in tonight."

"Don't think I'm doubting you," Bess said to Nancy as they continued back toward the bank, "but even you can't figure out a way to hide in that vault. You've seen what the security is like. Didn't you say Larry checked the whole place thoroughly before he closed the door last night?"

"He'll definitely see us," agreed George. "There's nowhere to hide."

"Yes there is," Nancy countered. "I just haven't figured it out yet."

"Nancy, how can you act completely sure about staying in the vault when you haven't even figured out how to get in there?" Bess demanded.

"But I will," Nancy assured her friends. "By five o'clock today I'll have come up with a solution. All we need is a little creative thinking."

"Didn't anyone ever tell you that some things are just impossible?" Bess said, pushing her point.

Nancy shook her head vehemently. "I can't accept that, Bess. This could be our only chance to catch the crooks in action. They already must have gotten through most of the deposit boxes. There can't be many left. And once they get what they're looking for, they're not going to stick around."

The girls climbed the broad marble steps leading up to the bank's entrance. "Make your own decision," Nancy said to her friends. "But if you're in, meet me in the lobby at five minutes to five."

As Nancy entered the bank, her mind kept churning. Age seemed to be the factor here. *Old* age. Was she missing someone, an obvious suspect she'd overlooked? She'd already talked to Larry Jaye and Evelyn Sobel. Was there someone else?

She gazed distractedly across the lobby. There, walking straight toward her and pushing a mop, was her answer. It was the janitor from the other night— Don, she remembered Mr. Charles calling him. His straight hair was mostly white, but Nancy could still see some strands of dark hair. The actor who'd played Jake in the movie had had black hair, but Nancy knew this didn't prove anything. Often actors looked nothing like the real people they portrayed.

Nancy decided a casual approach might work best. "How did the clean-up by the vault go yesterday?" she asked, flashing a friendly smile.

The janitor looked up, surprised. He seemed to have been lost in thought. "Excuse me," he said politely. "Do I know you?"

"I'm sorry," Nancy said. "I thought you might recognize me. I'm Nancy, the new intern here. I was the one who was downstairs when the tear gas exploded."

The janitor shrugged. "That was some mess. You know, it didn't say anything in my contract about tear gas. Just mopping and vacuuming and emptying ashtrays." He moved forward a few feet to mop a new area. Nancy followed.

"Have you been working here long?" she asked.

"Twenty years," the janitor said without looking up. He moved forward again. Was he trying to avoid her, Nancy wondered, or was he just doing his job?

"I guess you must know this bank inside and out," she said, following him.

"I've cleaned every room in this place at least five thousand times," the older man answered. He jangled a metal ring, heavy with keys, that hung from a loop on his overalls.

"Do you clean *all* the offices?" she inquired.

"Of course I do," he said irritably. "They never hired anybody to help me. I asked them about a million times, said it was too much for just one person, but—"

"Ahem." A woman cleared her throat right next to Nancy's ear.

Turning, Nancy found herself staring into the bifocals that rested on the sharp nose of Evelyn Sobel. Out of the corner of her eye Nancy saw the janitor rapidly mopping his way away from her and toward the opposite end of the lobby.

"Ms. Drew," Ms. Sobel said, "I have been looking for you for the past hour. Where have you been?"

"Mr. Charles sent me on an errand," Nancy explained. "Can I help you with anything?"

"You can do what you were hired to do, which is *work,*" Ms. Sobel said, her voice curt. "Come with me, please. I have a job for you."

92

Nancy smiled as she followed Evelyn Sobel up the stairs. This would be the perfect opportunity to find out more about the assistant branch manager without seeming like a snoop. Ms. Sobel led Nancy down the long hallway and opened the door to an empty conference room. In it was a large mahogany table surrounded by plush upholstered chairs. On the table was a box of blank envelopes and a tall stack of paper.

Ms. Sobel walked over to the table and laid one hand on the papers. "Do you know what a CD is?" she asked.

"Sure. It's a certificate of deposit," Nancy answered. "It's like a savings bond. For a certain sum of money— say, a thousand dollars—the bank agrees to pay a certain percentage of interest after a specific period of time has passed, for example, six months or a year."

Ms. Sobel didn't exactly smile, but the disapproving look on her face relaxed just a little. "Precisely," she confirmed. "And when the CD matures—that means when the money has sat in our bank for its stated amount of time—we have to remind our customers to buy a new CD or use the money in some other way." Ms. Sobel lifted the top paper off the stack. "These reminder forms have already been filled out," she told Nancy. "Your job is to stick the address labels on the envelopes and put the forms inside. I'll be back at five to five."

Without another word, Ms. Sobel left the room.

Nancy sighed, realizing she was stuck. She'd hoped to spend the rest of the afternoon questioning suspects. Instead, she was trapped here doing just about the most boring job the world had ever known! And if she didn't get it done, she'd blow her cover completely. Well, there was nothing she could do about it now. Resignedly, she sat down and folded the top form.

As Nancy removed a gummed label from a sheet and applied it to an envelope, she thought back to her conversation with the janitor. He hadn't been friendly at all. In fact, he'd seemed to be deliberately avoiding her. Then there was his key ring. If he cleaned all the offices, that had to include the president's. Mr. Charles probably hadn't remembered the janitor had a key when he'd said his was the only one. What's more, if the janitor had access to all the rooms, he might have been able to collect quite a lot of important information when no one was looking.

Nancy couldn't help wondering if it had been a coincidence that Ms. Sobel had interrupted her conversation with the janitor. If Ms. Sobel and Don the janitor were Jasmine and Jake, then Ms. Sobel would do everything in her power to keep Nancy from questioning her husband.

Nancy sighed. There was so much important investigating to be done, and she was stuck stuffing envelopes. Still, she could put the time to good use. Her hands might be busy, but her mind was free to work on the case. Now all she had to do was solve the impossible problem and figure out how three teenagers could sneak into a top security bank vault for a night!

There had to be a clue somewhere, something that seemed so ordinary that she'd missed it completely. She had to imagine every detail in the basement, check it as thoroughly in her thoughts as Larry did in fact each evening. In her mind's eye she pictured Larry opening the second gate and stepping into the steel-lined vault. Carefully, he'd peer into each corner of the room . . .

But after her mental investigation, Nancy felt just as satisfied that the vault was secure as Larry had the night before. She could imagine him nodding in approval, then swinging his small duffel bag over his shoulder and ducking into the viewing cubicle to change.

Suddenly Nancy let out a gasp. That was the answer! Larry used the cubicle as his own personal secret spot. There were no cameras and no guards in it. Why couldn't she, Bess, and George do the same?

Nancy felt like throwing her neat pile of stuffed envelopes high in the air and watching them shower down like confetti. One major piece of the puzzle had just fallen into place. Now she could use it to stake out the vault—and maybe that would lead to a full solution of this impossible mystery. Nancy reached for yet another envelope. It was amazing how the boring work suddenly didn't seem so bad now that she had the night in the vault to look forward to.

By five to five, when Evelyn Sobel returned, Nancy had acquired three paper cuts, and she thought she'd go delirious if she ever saw another CD renewal form, but all the envelopes were stuffed, sealed, and neatly stacked.

"Very good," Ms. Sobel said, tapping the mahogany desk loudly. "Maybe if you spent more time working and less time talking, you'd actually be an asset to this bank." Ms. Sobel laughed. "I just made a joke. An asset to this bank. I must write that down."

Nancy looked up at the assistant branch manager in surprise. She'd never expected to hear Ms. Sobel laugh. "May I go now?" she asked.

Ms. Sobel waved her away, and Nancy hurried from the conference room. She wasn't sure, but as she stepped out the door, she thought she heard the older woman murmur a quiet, "Thank you." *That* was even more astonishing than the laugh!

But Nancy had more important things to think about now—like the stakeout.

Her heart tapped out a pounding beat inside her chest as she hurried to where Bess and George were waiting for her at the top of the basement stairwell. "Glad you two decided to come in on this one with me," she said softly.

"Did you figure out how to hide us down there?" George asked.

"Sure did," Nancy replied proudly. Quickly, she filled them in on the plan. "I'll go down there first," she finished. "Wait at the turn in the stairs so you can see me, but don't let Larry catch sight of you. Come down when I give the signal." She wasn't quite sure how she'd sneak them all past Larry, so she'd just have to improvise.

Nancy started down the steps. The plan was scary, even dangerous, but they just had to do it. It was their best chance for solving the case! Steeling her courage, Nancy walked boldly past the electric eye to the outer gate.

Larry was standing behind his desk, taking his blue uniform jacket off the back of his chair.

"Hi, Larry. I guess it's almost closing time," Nancy commented with a smile.

"Nothing wrong with that," Larry said, returning the smile. "No bad effects from the tear gas, I hope?"

The guard unlocked the outer gate so Nancy could enter the area by his desk. She was relieved when he didn't reclose the gate behind her. Obviously, his thoughts were more on leaving for the day than on maintaining the bank's security.

"I'm fine," Nancy said in answer to Larry's question. "Actually, I came down to see how *you* were feeling. I wanted to ask you this morning, but we got distracted."

Larry leaned down to pick up his maroon duffel bag. "Isn't that sweet of you to ask! In fact, I'm feeling healthy and strong." He slapped his fist lightly against his chest. "At least as healthy as an old man like me is going to feel."

"Good," Nancy said, but she was reminded once again of the theme of old age which seemed so important in the case.

"Well, Nancy," Larry said, "I wish I had a few more minutes to visit with you, but it's time for me to close up here. Maurice should be coming down any minute, if he isn't late again. I want to check the vault and get out of here on time for once." With a little salute, Larry unlocked the inner gate and entered the vault.

Nancy watched as he went through his usual routine. He studied the empty room carefully, then nodded, satisfied. Quickly, he popped his head into each of the viewing cubicles and deemed them secure too. Then, gripping his duffel bag, he stepped into the last one and closed the door.

Nancy's heart gave a little leap. This was their chance! She motioned vigorously with her hand, and her friends silently appeared at her side.

Mouthing the words "come on," Nancy tiptoed across the vault's marble floor and slipped into the end cubicle. Ignoring the panic in Bess's eyes, she ushered the girls in with her. Without a sound she closed the door behind them.

It was eerily dark in the cubicle, but a few stray rays of light squeezed their way in through the cracks around the door frame. Nancy could just make out the shadowy outlines of her friends. If Larry heard them, the stakeout was finished and the chance of solving the mystery probably gone. The seconds stretched out like hours as the three friends waited nervously.

Crickkk. The noise was faint, but Nancy recognized it as the sound of the far cubicle's door swinging open.

Then the echo of footsteps clicked across the marble floor. Larry was leaving! They were safe—at least until the thieves showed up. *If* they showed up.

Then the sound of a second set of footsteps clattered through the vault. These steps sounded energetic, younger than Larry's more subdued gait. What was going on? Yet another strange emergency in the vault?

The footsteps stopped.

"Sorry I'm late." Nancy recognized the breathless voice of Maurice Grun.

"I don't know why you even bother to apologize anymore," Larry said gruffly. "You're late every day."

"Did you check the vault yet?" Maurice asked.

"If you'd gotten here when you were supposed to, you would have known I did."

"Cubicles too?"

"Yep."

"I know it's my fault I'm late," Maurice said apologetically, "but I'm supposed to watch you check everything. Could you do it again?"

Check the cubicles again? Nancy's heart almost stopped.

"Maurice," Larry said, his voice tight with anger. "I'm sick and tired of you making me do everything twice."

But when Nancy heard Larry's footsteps crossing the vault again, she realized he wasn't going to stand up to the head teller. She and her friends were sunk! She held her breath, knowing they would be discovered, as the far cubicle's door was pulled open. They were next.

"Maurice!" Nancy heard another man call. Mr. Charles's voice resounded against the steel walls. His tone revealed the same controlled fury she had seen in him the evening before. "Why hasn't the vault been closed? And these gates are wide open. We've had enough trouble down here without you adding to it. Is Larry done inside?"

In the semidarkness, Nancy saw the doorknob of their cubicle start to turn. She exchanged an anxious look with Bess and George.

"Yes, Mr. Charles," the girls heard Larry say. His voice was so close, they could practically hear him breathing.

"Well, then, get out here." Mr. Charles sounded very annoyed. "I want this place locked up!"

The doorknob released back to its original position. A second later Nancy heaved a sigh of relief as she heard Larry's footsteps moving away. The light in the main vault room clicked off and the girls were left in total darkness. In a moment they'd be locked in. In a moment they'd have accomplished the first part of their plan!

But even though she expected it, the next sound sent a cold chill through Nancy's usually fearless heart. It was the heavy clang of the vault door shutting them in for the night.

There was a creaking sound as the metal wheel outside the door locked twenty-four steel tumblers into place. Then there was absolute silence.

There was no way anyone could hear them now. Not if they shouted in victory or if they screamed for help. Still, Nancy waited several more minutes before she spoke. When she did, it was barely more than a whisper. "Well, we did it," she said to her friends, her voice quavering slightly. "What did I tell you? You've got to think creatively."

She reached above, feeling for the light switch. Her hand slid along the smooth wooden wall until it hit the switch. Then she flicked it on. Overhead, a naked light bulb cast a harsh glow over the three of them. They found themselves in a tiny wood-paneled room. A wooden ledge projected from the wall like a desk, and a wooden chair was pushed up against it. Quickly, Bess dropped into the chair and stretched her legs out, leaving Nancy and George to make do with the floor. "Well, at least one of us ought to be comfortable," she explained.

Nancy planned for her friends and herself to stay in the cubicle, remaining hidden from the thieves. That way, they could learn the criminals' identities without endangering themselves. At least, she *hoped* that was the way it would work.

"I hope we don't starve in here." Bess was grumbling again.

Nancy laughed. "We'll be out of here when Larry comes into work tomorrow morning, exactly sixteen hours from now. That's not long enough to starve. Human beings can go for *days* without food."

Bess looked horrified at the thought. "Well, we still could have planned it better. We should have picked up some sandwiches at Kathy's to tide us over."

"Here." Nancy reached into her purse, feeling around for an extra candy bar she remembered stashing there. She pulled it out and handed it to Bess. "Chocolate almond. That should give you plenty of energy."

"Actually, I'm less concerned with eating than I am with breathing," said George. "Are you absolutely sure we won't suffocate in here?"

"I checked that out thoroughly," Nancy reassured them. "There's an air vent in each cubicle and one in the main room. I guess the bank wanted a safeguard in case anyone ever got locked in by accident."

"Thank goodness," Bess said, inhaling deeply. "But Nancy, what are we going to do while we wait? If the hunger doesn't get us, the boredom will!"

Bess was right, Nancy realized. She'd been so excited about the stakeout that she hadn't even considered how long and tedious the evening might get. "Too bad there's no VCR in here," she said. "I still have the *Jake and Jasmine* video in my purse."

"You mean, 'Watch the video, then see it live'?" Bess quipped. "Nancy, it's going to be a *long* night."

"I also have a pack of cards in my purse," Nancy said. "That will help pass the time."

For the next couple of hours the girls played Crazy Eights, Go Fish, and War, until even Nancy couldn't face a rematch.

"Why don't you both try to sleep," Nancy finally suggested. "There's no reason for all of us to sweat it out, as long as one of us stays awake. I'll take the first shift."

"I'll take the next one," George volunteered. "Wake me when you're tired." The cousins stretched out on the floor, using their bags for pillows. Bess draped her jacket around her as a blanket. Within a few minutes both of them lay fast asleep. Nancy couldn't understand how they did it. Though she herself felt totally drained from the danger of the past two days, she was much too excited to sleep. She was getting too close to a solution.

Without Bess and George's company, the time passed slowly. Nancy could feel her own eyes beginning to droop, but she let her friends continue dreaming. She didn't want to risk missing anything by taking a sleeping shift herself.

"Any minute now," she kept repeating to herself. "Any minute . . ."

Only when a sound startled her out of her dreams did Nancy realize she'd allowed herself to fall asleep. She rubbed her eyes hastily. Something was happening, and she couldn't afford to be groggy. Once again the creaking sound cut into the silent night. The wheel that kept the vault shut—someone was turning it!

Nancy checked her watch. The quartz crystal blinked 1:21 back at her. She smiled to herself ruefully; certainly long past normal banking hours. She wanted desperately to alert Bess and George, but she couldn't risk them talking or asking questions out loud in the first few moments after she woke them.

Quickly, she reached up and flicked off the overhead light. In the dark silence Nancy realized her heart was pounding madly.

The creaking split the night for a third time. Nancy pushed the cubicle door ajar just a crack. Peering through, she watched breathlessly as the vault door began to open.

12

A Deadly Poison

The vault's heavy door eased open on its silent hinges. Nancy shivered. She was about to learn the identity of the criminals!

From her post at the crack in the door, all she could see was a thin sliver of the larger room. Then a foot in a black leather sneaker stepped into view. The step made no sound on the marble floor. Part of the figure—but not the face—moved into her line of vision. It was a woman, Nancy realized from the body's shape, and she was wearing a black trench coat and black gloves.

Come on, come on, Nancy urged silently. Just one more step and she'd see the face.

Then the figure did move, but the woman's identity had been carefully concealed beneath a dark ski mask. Nancy felt like screaming in frustration.

Soon a second black-clad figure joined the first in the little slot of space that Nancy could see. This one was a man, and like his partner, he'd hidden his face with a ski mask. He carried a large black canvas bag under one arm.

Nancy scrutinized the pair, but she could make out no identifying traits. They did walk rather slowly. Were they just being careful or was it an indication of old age? It was hard to tell.

The couple headed straight for the corner of the vault where the video camera hung. Nancy could tell from their lack of hesitation that they'd done all this before. The man pulled a small folding stepladder out of the bag. Setting it beneath the camera, he climbed up and pulled a screwdriver from his pocket. In less than a minute the camera lay open before him.

He wrenched the old video cassette from it while the woman pulled a second cassette from the nylon bag and handed it to him. The man quickly set it into place, shut the camera, and screwed the bolts back in.

All through the operation, neither thief had made so much as a peep. Real professionals, Nancy decided.

As the woman pulled an enormous key ring from her pocket, though, the jangling echoed through the vault. Nancy realized she'd seen keys like that before—in Alan Charles's office safe. She'd been right when she'd figured the thieves had made copies of them.

Now the woman in black headed for the safe-deposit boxes on the same wall as the vault door. She searched through the keys on the ring until she found the one she wanted. Then she pushed it into the keyhole of one of the boxes. That took care of the box holder's key, but what about the second key kept by the bank?

Almost before Nancy could complete her thought, the man pulled a single key out of his pocket, inserted it into the same box, and pulled the door open.

Quickly, silently, and methodically, the man and

woman pulled out the steel drawer in the box and pawed through the contents. It didn't take the couple more than a few moments to realize this wasn't the box they were looking for. They closed it up and repeated the process with the next one.

Nancy bit her lip in frustration. Here she was, not more than ten feet from the criminals, watching them in action, and she hadn't learned a single thing she didn't already know. Who were they? What were they looking for? Those two questions echoed through her mind like the jangling of the key ring in the cavernous vault. The couple was just finishing their third box when suddenly the shrieking scream of an alarm slashed through the silence. It was the five-minute safeguard Mr. Charles had told her about—the alarm went off five minutes after the door was opened if anyone entered the vault after regular working hours. It was awful. The sound was so loud, Nancy felt as though a rocket were going off inside her brain. Instantly, Bess and George were up.

"Wha—" Bess yelped. Nancy clamped her hand down hard on Bess's mouth. She couldn't be sure, but she thought she saw the woman look toward their cubicle. Had she heard Bess's cry, or had the alarm drowned it out?

Meanwhile, the couple in black were panicking. Leaving the last safe-deposit box wide open, they threw their equipment back into the canvas bag. The door of the vault was slowly sliding closed on its mechanical hinges, and each instant they delayed brought them closer to being trapped.

Nancy watched as the man tossed the stepladder— the last piece of equipment—back into the bag, and the couple made a mad dash for the vault door. The ever-narrowing gap had shrunk to just about a foot.

The man squeezed through, the door grazing his stomach.

In that final, desperate moment, the woman turned and stared straight at the cubicle where the girls were hiding. Had she heard Bess? Or was she just looking over her shoulder to make sure she hadn't left anything behind? Nancy couldn't tell, but she knew it seemed wrong that the woman had hesitated at such a crucial moment. With only seconds to spare, the woman slipped through.

The vault door was just inches from closing. On the other side of it the man grabbed the woman in a relieved, impassioned embrace. As the heavy door slammed shut, Nancy heard him utter a single word. That word was *Jasmine*.

The moment the door closed tight, the deafening alarm shut off. Nancy still couldn't hear very clearly, though, because the ringing kept on going inside her ears.

"Oh, Nancy," Bess wailed. "I'm really sorry. I should have kept my big mouth shut. What if they heard me? What if they saw us?"

"Don't worry about it," Nancy said. "I doubt she heard anything except that awful ringing. I still can hardly hear you."

"I haven't felt this deaf since the Brain Waves played the River Heights Arena," said George. She pressed her ears with her fingers.

"Even if they did see us," Nancy said soothingly, "they can't come back for us now. They've already set off the alarm. The police and the night watchman should be here any minute."

"Did you hear him call her Jasmine?" Bess asked excitedly. "It's incredible, it was really them, Jake and Jasmine Sims!"

"But we still don't know who they are," Nancy said. "Obviously, they're not working at the bank under their real names. So who are they posing as?"

George sneezed. "That is still a mystery," she pronounced, then sneezed again. "Bess, are you wearing that new perfume again, the one I'm allergic to? What's it called, Donder? Blitzen?"

"Vixen," Bess said, annoyed. "And no, I'm not wearing it. Since I'm a nice cousin, I never wear it when I'm around you."

"Oh." George sniffed. "Well, something smells funny."

"Maybe we've all been in this room too long," Bess said. "Nancy is hearing alarms that have already shut off, and George is smelling perfume that isn't there."

Nancy pushed open the cubicle door to let in a little more air. "That should help," she said.

"No! No, it won't," George cried. She pointed, horrified, to the ceiling of the main room. High above them a plume of gray smoke was wafting down from the air vent.

"What is it?" Bess asked. Her voice shook with fear as the smoke started to pour in faster and thicker.

"It's coming from the vents in here too," George cried, waving a finger toward the air vent in their cubicle.

"Oh, Nancy, what should we do?" Bess said, practically sobbing.

"Get into the main room and stay low," Nancy shouted. "Pull your collars up over your mouths and breathe through the cloth."

Staying near the ground, the girls crawled out of the cubicle.

"It's even worse out here," Bess said, starting to cough.

George was coughing too. "I take it back," she said to her cousin. "This is even *worse* than Blitzen."

"Vixen!" shouted Bess, gasping.

Nancy found herself choking. The unbearable smell seemed to fill her lungs. It was as if someone had wrapped a heavy elastic band around her ribs and was pulling it tighter. Beside her, Bess and George were gagging.

"What's happening? What . . . is . . . it?" Bess asked weakly as she tried desperately to breathe.

The awful truth came to Nancy through a sickly haze. With her last bit of strength, Nancy tried to tell her friends the truth, but the words came out so quietly she was sure Bess and George didn't hear.

"It's poison gas," she whispered.

Then the world went black around her.

13

A Revealing Brand

At first there was nothing but darkness and a steady pounding. Deep inside a heavy fog, Nancy wondered where she was and where the pounding was coming from.

Gradually, she realized the awful thudding was inside her own head. Then she felt the pain. Her skull was throbbing so hard and loud, she was sure it would split wide open.

She thought she heard voices, but the pounding was too distracting to concentrate. In another moment everything faded as Nancy lost consciousness again.

The pounding had stopped, but the voices were still there. They were louder this time, clear and familiar.

"Oh, Mr. Drew," a woman's voice said anxiously, "why doesn't she wake up?"

Hannah! Nancy tried to open her eyes, but her lids felt too heavy. She tried to speak, but her lips seemed glued together.

"Nancy?" It was her father. "Can you hear me?"

Nancy felt a gentle pressure as her father placed his hand in hers. Using all her strength, she tried to squeeze his fingers. Once, twice, she wrapped her fingers around her father's.

Carson Drew let out a joyful cry. "She's awake!"

"Nancy!" Hannah moaned thankfully, "Oh, Nancy."

Focusing all her energy on her eyes, Nancy managed to crack them open just a slit. The afternoon light hit her like a sledgehammer, it was so bright. She could make out a high institutional bed and a row of charts. She was lying in a hospital bed, she realized.

"Nancy, oh darling," Carson said softly. "We're all here. Hannah and myself and Mr. Charles. And Bess and George are going to be okay too. They're right here in the other beds."

"I'm so thankful you're back," cried Hannah, dabbing at her eyes with a tissue. "We were so worried about you! The Faynes and the Marvins were here all night. We finally sent them home this morning to get some sleep."

"Dad," Nancy moaned. "Hannah."

Alan Charles stepped up to the bedside. "Nancy, that was a terrible stunt you pulled last night." His voice was anxious and concerned. "You all could have been killed!"

"Don't be so hard on her," said Hannah.

"I'm just as concerned as you are," Mr. Charles assured Hannah. "And I blame myself."

But Nancy didn't care about all that. "Did . . . you . . . catch . . . them?" Nancy managed to croak.

Carson Drew smiled. "She may be weak, but she hasn't lost interest in the case."

Mr. Charles leaned toward Nancy. "No, we didn't. In fact, the police almost made a terrible mistake. They wanted to arrest——"

Carson Drew cut him off. "We can tell her about that later."

Nancy wanted to ask Mr. Charles what he meant, but she felt too awful.

There was a knock on the door, which felt like a good hard rap on the head to Nancy. Hannah rose to get it. She opened the door just a crack. "Who is it?" she demanded, but Nancy couldn't catch the visitor's answer.

"Now, look here," Nancy heard Hannah say to the person on the other side of the door, "they're still too sick to talk to you. Why can't you come back tomorrow?"

"I'm sorry," said a woman's voice, "but I insist on seeing them immediately."

"Well, since you have that badge, I suppose I must!" Hannah replied heatedly. She stepped back and two police officers entered the room. The first was a short, commanding woman with bright red hair, which she'd tucked into her cap. The other Nancy recognized as Sergeant Ramirez, the friendly officer who had shown Nancy and her friends the computer at the police station. She managed a sickly smile, but the sergeant didn't return it.

"I'm Captain Elizabeth Steiner," the woman officer said, striding purposefully toward Nancy's bed.

Summoning all her strength, Nancy nodded hello to the officer.

"That's her!" exclaimed Sergeant Ramirez. "The one I told you about yesterday."

Steiner looked grimly at Nancy. "Ms. Drew, I must

111

inform you that you are under arrest! You have the right to remain silent . . ." she began.

So this was what her father and Mr. Charles had been talking about! The police thought she and George and Bess were the burglars! If she hadn't been so sick, Nancy would have laughed. Here, the captain was telling her she had the right to remain silent when she was too weak even to talk.

"Anything you say—"

"Whoa, wait a minute," Nancy's father cut in. "I thought we cleared this up last night."

Captain Steiner droned on, "Anything you say can be used against you in a court of law."

"Stop!" cried Mr. Charles. "I told you already, I refuse to file any charges against these girls. They work for me and were doing an investigation by my request."

Sergeant Ramirez looked questioningly at Mr. Charles, then frowned. "And we told you that if there was something illegal going on, you should have come to us."

"It's very complicated," Mr. Charles told him. "But I'll be happy to answer any questions you might have, as will the girls, once they're feeling a little stronger."

Captain Steiner looked suspiciously from Nancy to Bess to George as they lay in their beds. "I guess that will have to do," she agreed reluctantly. "But in the meantime, I'm going to station Sergeant Ramirez outside the door." She threw Nancy a not very sympathetic frown. "As soon as you're able, we must have your cooperation." Then she strode from the room with Sergeant Ramirez right behind her.

Nancy shook her head, feeling annoyed. How could the police come up with the ridiculous conclusion that the girls were the crooks? Even though they *were* in the vault, they hardly would have poisoned themselves!

"Tell . . . me . . . details," Nancy croaked to Mr. Charles.

Mr. Charles let out a heavy sigh. "I'm still not sure exactly what happened," he said, shaking his head. "Last night, around quarter after one, my beeper went off, telling me there was a break-in at the vault. I ran right over and got there at the same time as the police. I had to call Evelyn Sobel in order to get inside the vault. That's when we found the three of you unconscious. I'm only glad we got you out of there in time."

"Poison," Nancy said.

"I know," said Alan Charles. "We found the gas container inside the air vent in the basement. They must have set it off before they escaped. Well, they certainly came prepared. Whoever they are."

"We . . . saw . . . them," Nancy said hoarsely. "But . . . masked."

A mixture of surprise and excitement, tingled with a desire for revenge, swept over Mr. Charles's face as he leaned toward Nancy. "Who?" he demanded. "Who were they?"

"VCR," Nancy said ambiguously. The effort to speak was exhausting her. "Must watch . . . movie."

"But there's nothing on the security videotape," Mr. Charles replied, his excitement turning instantly to disappointment.

"No!" Nancy said with the last of her strength. It was *Jake and Jasmine* she wanted to see. If she knew a little more about the Simses' younger lives, maybe it would give her the clue she needed to crack this case. She tried to prop herself up on one elbow, but she couldn't manage it. Her head fell back into her pillow and she closed her eyes.

"Enough!" she heard her father say. "She needs her rest."

113

Nancy heard their chairs scrape against the floor as they got up to go. She tried desperately to call out after them, to tell them that she had to see the rest of *Jake and Jasmine*.

"Dad . . ." Nancy called feebly, but it was too late. Her visitors had gone. She felt too weak even to open her eyes. I'll just lie here a minute, she thought. Just for a minute . . .

In far less time, Nancy was sound asleep.

Nancy shook her reddish blond hair groggily and eased her eyes open. The poison was slowly working itself out of her system, and she felt much better now. She knew her blood was pumping more strongly in her veins. She stretched her arms up. Her muscles, too, were coming back to life.

Now she took a good look at her surroundings. The hospital room sparkled with cleanliness. A large vase with bright flowers stood on a table by the bed, probably a gift from her father. Near them lay a box of tissues, a paperback novel one of her visitors must have left behind, and her purse. Good. They must have found her bag when they'd pulled her and her friends out of the vault.

She reached for it, then fished around inside until she found her watch. The quartz read 9:04, and the darkness outside told her that meant P.M., not A.M. So she'd been asleep almost a day. Nancy suddenly realized she felt very hungry.

But there was something more pressing right now than food. She had to see the rest of *Jake and Jasmine*. It had provided her with a key clue before. She just hoped something even more conclusive would show up in the final hour of the film. She felt again in her purse.

114

Yes, the cassette was still in there. She grasped its square corner and pulled it out.

With only a little effort Nancy pulled herself up to a sitting position. She felt slightly dizzy, but otherwise okay. Throwing back the covers, she placed her bare feet on the cold floor. So far so good.

"Ohhh," came a groan directly in front of her. It was Bess, shifting painfully under the covers.

"Bess?" Nancy approached her friend's bed. "Are you okay?"

"My stomach," Bess moaned.

"Does it hurt?" Nancy asked, concerned.

"No, it's empty!" Bess said. Then she blinked open her eyes. "Mom and Dad were here already," she murmured, half to herself. "I guess I must have fallen asleep again."

"Nancy?" came a weak call from across the room. "Bess?"

Nancy padded over to George's bed. "Thank goodness we're all awake at one time again," she said, taking her friend's hand reassuringly.

"Thank goodness we're awake at all!" George exclaimed. "Wow. The Simses sure use strong ammunition."

"I know," Nancy agreed, nodding. "But I'm determined to crack the secret of their identity."

"How?" Bess wanted to know. She ran a hand through her blond hair.

"I'm not sure," Nancy replied. "But if we can find a VCR, maybe this movie will give us some clues." She held up the cassette.

"And we'll have a little *safe* entertainment," Bess agreed, "instead of all this traipsing around bank vaults during robberies."

"So . . . let's go," George said, sitting up in her bed.

Nancy stepped waveringly toward the door. Suddenly she stopped, remembering foggily the events that had occurred earlier in the hospital room. "There's just one tiny little problem," she informed her friends. She pointed to the door. "Sergeant Ramirez is sitting right outside. We're being guarded."

"From the crooks?" Bess asked. "That's a very good idea."

"No," Nancy explained. "The police think *we're* the crooks."

"Us?" George cried. "That's ridiculous!"

"Think about it," Nancy said. "Whom did they find—illegally, I might add—in the vault when the alarm went off?"

Bess cut in. "But Mr. Charles could tell them—"

"He already did," Nancy said. "If we're lucky, they won't arrest us. But they're dying to question us. And that could take up valuable time. If Jake and Jasmine haven't already left town, I'm sure they will any minute. We've got to find a VCR without Sergeant Ramirez seeing us."

George pushed herself out of bed and tiptoed over to the door. Very quietly she opened it a few inches. The dark blue back of Sergeant Ramirez's uniform was visible just outside the room. Hastily George pushed the door shut again. "Trapped!" she said glumly.

"Not necessarily," Bess said. She picked up the phone.

"What are you doing?" Nancy asked.

Bess spoke into the phone. "Is this the operator? Yes, I'm calling from the Bentley police station. I'd like to page a Sergeant Ramirez, please. Very urgent police business."

Bess held up the receiver and flashed a conspiratorial smile at her friends. "See, just like Nancy said, all you have to do is think creatively!"

Within seconds they heard a voice blast over a loudspeaker in the hall. "Sergeant Ramirez, pick up on extension seventy-seven. Sergeant Ramirez."

The girls heard the chair shift outside their door, followed by the sound of footsteps receding down the hall. Opening the door again, George peeked out for a second time. "He's gone!" she said in an excited whisper.

"Great thinking, Bess," Nancy said. "Keep him on the phone. Tell him you're calling for Captain Steiner and that she's taking another phone call. Ask him to hold the line. Then come find us."

Bess gave them the okay signal, and Nancy and George sped out into the hallway. To their right, a few yards down, Nancy spotted the nurses' station. "This way," she said, heading for it with George right behind her. A young nurse with a round face and long black hair was filling out some forms behind the desk. Her name tag read S. Sun.

"Excuse us," Nancy said politely. The nurse looked up and smiled. "Is there a VCR on this floor?" Nancy asked.

"Patients' lounge." Nurse Sun pointed to the end of the corridor. "But I think someone's using it right now."

"Thank you," Nancy said, and she and George started to walk away.

"Hey, wait a minute!" Nurse Sun called after them.

Nancy turned slowly. Had Sergeant Ramirez informed the hospital staff that the girls were under suspicion? Was Nurse Sun going to send her and George straight back to bed?

The nurse reached under the counter and pulled up

two pairs of disposable slippers. "Put these on," she advised. "You don't want to catch pneumonia while you're in the hospital!"

Nancy let out a laugh. Then, thanking the nurse, the girls put on the slippers and shuffled toward the end of the hall.

The patients' lounge was empty except for a young woman sitting on an orange couch. She was thin and wore a hospital gown, a robe, and big black glasses. Her frizzy blond hair was pulled up in a huge, puffy ponytail on top of her head. When the girls came in, she didn't even look up, just continued to stare fixedly at the color TV. On screen, a spaceship swooshed past a galaxy of stars. A VCR was whirring on the shelf beneath the TV.

"Excuse me," Nancy began.

"Shhh," the woman told her without looking up. "Can't you see I'm watching?"

"I don't mean to interrupt," Nancy said firmly, "but this is very important."

The woman pressed the pause button on the VCR remote and turned to Nancy with a long, unfriendly face.

"We need to watch this movie," Nancy explained, holding up her cassette. "It could help us catch two bank robbers who've been eluding the police for almost thirty years."

The woman laughed. "Sure. And I need to watch *Star Base* so I can catch the man on the moon!"

Nancy bit her lip. She wasn't sure what to do now to convince the woman to give up the VCR. So it was with surprise that she watched the woman push herself out of the couch and eject the *Star Base* cassette. "That's such a good story, you deserve a few points for creativity! I can watch *Star Base* later. Mind if I watch your movie too? This is something I've got to see for myself."

"No problem," Nancy told the woman. "Oh, and thanks!" Then, with shaking fingers, she loaded *Jake and Jasmine* into the machine. A moment later Bess tiptoed into the room, settling into the couch next to George and the other patient.

Nancy pressed the play button and the film picked up where the video-store woman had switched it off. Jake and Jasmine were beginning their first joy ride in the 1957 white convertible Skyliner.

Part of the storyline wasn't too different from a lot of romantic movies. Jasmine defied her father's demand that she stop seeing Jake. But even though the movie itself was pretty hokey, Nancy had to admit that there was something special about Jake—his daring, his abandon. Nancy could really understand Jasmine's fascination with this charming, handsome young man. It was the night of the prom, the story revealed, when Jasmine made her big decision to follow Jake in his life of crime. Her father had locked her in her room while all her friends went off to the dance. Jake climbed up the vines that clung to the side of her house and whisked her away from all that.

In the next half hour Nancy learned that Jake and Jasmine had started small, robbing stores and gas stations. Then they'd become bolder and began to go after banks. In between holdups Jake was always trying to prove his love for Jasmine, buying her flowers and expensive gifts. No matter what he did, though, it wasn't enough. Jasmine always threatened to leave him and go straight. Finally, Jake decided to make the final gesture. He blindfolded Jasmine and drove her to a tattoo parlor. Then he made her watch while he had his right forearm imprinted with dye. Nancy let out a

119

gasp as the camera zoomed in for a close-up of the new tattoo. A many-petaled, pale yellow flower stood out in stark relief against Jake's skin. Underneath the flower was the word *Jasmine*.

Nancy knew exactly where she'd seen that design before. On the right forearm of Larry Jaye!

14

Who Is Jasmine?

So, Larry was actually Jake Sims! One of the area's most legendary bank robbers was the number-one guard at the bank's vault!

Nancy pressed the stop button on the VCR and ejected her cassette. "Thank you," she said to the woman with the puffy ponytail. "Sorry to interrupt your show."

"Well? Did you figure out who did it?" the woman asked.

Nancy nodded. Bess and George shot her identical amazed stares. "Well, thanks for telling us!" said Bess. "Who is it? What did you find out?"

Nancy pressed her lips together. She didn't want to say anything in front of the other woman. "You know," she said instead, "I'm feeling a little hungry. I wonder if we could get a couple of dinner trays at this hour." She shuffled toward the door in her hospital slippers, the cassette tucked under her arm.

Bess and George followed quickly after her.

"Come on, Nancy, out with it," George said.

Nancy shook her head, then motioned with it toward the woman in the lounge, who was already engrossed again in *Star Base*. Nodding to show they understood, Bess and George silently followed Nancy out of the lounge.

Peering down the hall, Nancy could see no sign of Sergeant Ramirez outside their room. There was just an empty chair with a paperback book on it. Nancy was sure he wasn't still holding the line. In fact, when he'd discovered the call was a fake, he probably checked their room and discovered they were gone. Now he was most likely tearing the hospital apart looking for them. As soon as they were safely back inside, Nancy shut the door.

"It's Larry," she told her friends. "Larry Jaye is Jake Sims!"

"Wow," George said, shaking her head, "and he seemed so friendly and innocent."

Nancy went on to describe Larry's tattoo. "I didn't think anything of it at the time," she told them, "and I couldn't read the name below the flower. But I'm positive it's the same design."

"Who would have thought that exciting young man would turn into a regular-looking guy like Larry," Bess commented.

"It makes sense, though," Nancy said slowly. "Larry told me he was from a tiny town in the middle of nowhere, but he wouldn't reveal the name of it. He also said he'd had a wild youth, but he was pretty secretive about the details. Now I can see why."

"It all fits," Bess agreed. "But I still have one question. Who is Jasmine?"

Nancy shook her head. "Larry would need an accomplice at the bank in order to get all the information and keys he'd need. So it's a good bet that Jasmine's working at the bank under a false name too."

"What about Evelyn Sobel?" George suggested. "She's about the same age as Larry, and she's got access to all the information in the bank's computers."

"Her behavior *is* strange," Nancy admitted. "Especially the part about her visiting the vault so often. But there are a couple of things that don't feel right. First of all, we still can't explain how she got into Mr. Charles's safe to get the duplicate keys to the safe-deposit boxes. Mr. Charles swears no one but he himself knows the combination."

"But Ms. Sobel's the assistant branch manager," George reasoned. "She must spend a lot of time with Mr. Charles. Maybe she spied on him while he was opening the safe."

"I doubt Mr. Charles would have been that careless," Nancy said. "The other problem I have is with the glove. It may actually be Ms. Sobel's, but it seems like a very obvious plant. I'm convinced the real Jasmine left it in Mr. Charles's office to set Ms. Sobel up."

"Which brings us back to my question," Bess said. "Who is the real Jasmine?"

Nancy shook her head. She didn't have any other older woman suspects on her list. "There's only one way to find out." She walked over to the room's small closet. "Let's get dressed. We need to investigate!"

"Where are we going?" George asked.

"To Larry's house," Nancy replied. "I wrote his home address down when George was working on the bank's computer. Let's get over there. Even if Larry and Jasmine aren't there themselves, it's the most likely place to find more clues."

"Oh boy," Bess said, rolling her eyes. "You sure do

have this funny habit. Someone tries to kill you and almost succeeds. Then, when you're safe, you go out of your way to put yourself back in the line of fire."

"You don't have to come if you don't want to," Nancy said.

"I'm not chickening out," Bess assured her. "I'm just pointing out a fact. And there's one more thing."

Nancy pulled her red dress over her head, then looked quizzically at Bess. "What's that?"

"Well, technically, we shouldn't be leaving the hospital because they haven't checked us out yet. Don't you think we should wait until a doctor says it's okay?"

"Look," Nancy said as she threw on her black blazer over the dress, "Sergeant Ramirez is probably combing the hospital for us. We've got to leave now, before he catches us."

"I'm with you, Nancy," George declared. She hurriedly discarded her hospital gown and pulled on her skirt and blouse. Reluctantly, Bess did the same.

Nancy reached into her purse for her notebook. Flipping it open, she found Larry's address. "Two twenty-two Lakeview Drive," she murmured aloud. "I think I know where that is." She tossed the notebook on the bed and grabbed her car keys from her purse.

"Everybody ready?" she asked.

Bess and George nodded. "As ready as I'll ever be," Bess added.

"Okay, then. Let's go." She pushed open the door and checked the hallway.

"All clear," she whispered. "But don't run, so no one gets suspicious."

The ten yards of hallway to the back stairway seemed endless. Every second of the way Nancy was sure Sergeant Ramirez was going to come flying down the hall, waving his handcuffs. Then they'd all be hauled

124

down to the police station, and they'd never catch Jake and Jasmine. It seemed miraculous that by the time they reached the exit he still hadn't appeared.

As soon as they were safely inside the stairwell, the girls broke into a run. Nancy could see that her friends still felt a little shaky, as she did herself, but they scooted down the two flights of stairs at their very fastest pace. Within a few minutes they were pushing open the door to the lobby. Nancy glanced quickly around. No Sergeant Ramirez. No angry nurse demanding that the girls get back in bed until the doctor gave the word. Their escape had been all too easy, Nancy thought as she led Bess and George toward the main door.

"Wait a minute, girls," said a loud voice. Nancy felt a heavy hand on her shoulder. Trying to remain calm, she turned around.

A huge woman in a flowered dress stood before them, clutching a glossy hospital brochure. "Can you tell me how to get to Pediatrics?" she asked in a booming, shrill voice. "My nephew just got his tonsils out, and I can't find the right department. I've been wandering around for fifteen minutes, trying to read this map, but it's too confusing!"

A wave of relief flushed Nancy's cheeks. Then, quickly, it was replaced by a flash of annoyance. She smiled as politely as she could, but right now every extra second they stayed around put her and her friends in more danger.

"I'm afraid I don't know where it is," she replied. "Maybe one of the nurses can help you."

"Thank you," the woman said, wandering off.

Breathing a sigh of relief, Nancy, Bess, and George filed through the revolving door and emerged into the starry night. The redbrick towers of Bentley General

Hospital were silhouetted against the darkness behind them. The girls walked along the curving driveway and onto Main Street. Across the street, Vera's World of Video was now dark and empty. Down the street stood the Bentley Bank.

Nancy hurried toward the elegant white building. "I parked the car right in front of the bank yesterday when we went to work. I hope it's still there." Breaking into a run, she took off down the street.

"Slow down!" Bess called from behind her. "Remember, we were poisoned less than twenty-four hours ago!"

Nancy didn't have to be told to go slower. She was feeling a lot more tired than she normally would have. Her legs wobbled beneath her and she gasped for air. Bess and George sped after her, also breathing heavily.

"I hate feeling like this—so weak and vulnerable," Nancy cried in a rare display of anger.

"It will pass soon," George said, placing a hand on Nancy's shoulder. "It's amazing we're up at all."

Nancy spotted her blue sports car waiting for them in front of the bank, right where she'd left it. She unlocked the doors and the three of them piled in. In another moment they were speeding over the crest of the hill and down the steep slope on the other side. Within ten minutes they were cruising down Lakeview Drive.

"Pretty fancy neighborhood for a bank guard to be living in," Nancy commented. Stately old homes lined either side of the street, and Nancy noticed a new car or two in more than a few of the driveways. The lake's black waters reflected the light of the lamp posts.

"Check the numbers for me," Nancy told Bess.

Bess squinted through the window. "It's hard to see. Oh wait, there's 194 . . . 200 . . . 208 . . ."

"I think we'd better walk the rest of the way," Nancy suggested. "They might notice the car."

Nancy pulled over and parked on the incline, and the girls got out of the car. They didn't have to walk more than another block to reach number 222.

Larry's place was a large one-story house with a wooden porch. A picture window took up most of the front wall. Light poured out of it, and Nancy noticed the glow of a TV set. Great! Jake and Jasmine hadn't made their getaway yet. Probably they figured Nancy, Bess, and George were dead and that they didn't have to worry about being tagged as the robbers.

Nancy took in the idyllic scene. It was hard to believe such a pleasant house was the home of two notorious criminals. They'd be furious when they realized the girls were still alive. Nancy was sure they wouldn't hesitate to correct the situation if they discovered the three of them.

"Try not even to breathe," Nancy cautioned the others as she crept toward Jake's gravel driveway. "We can't afford to make a single sound." Nancy stayed off the gravel—too noisy—and kept to the lawn. At the far end of the driveway she could make out a single-car garage.

"That's probably where they keep the Skyliner," George whispered, pointing.

"Let's check it out after we look through the house." Silently, Nancy sneaked up to the porch. "Stay low," she cautioned, "so they can't spot us through the window."

The girls crept beneath the plate glass. Then, very slowly, they raised their heads above the level of the windowsill to get a good look inside.

They were home! Nancy immediately recognized the back of Larry's head. He sat on a sofa with his back to the closed window. A gray-haired woman snuggled next to him—Jasmine, Nancy figured. But it was the bunch of keys sitting in plain view on the end of the table that really made her smile. It was the key ring they'd used to open the safe-deposit boxes. Great! That was hard evidence, and all Nancy would need to get a good solid conviction in a court of law.

Now Nancy turned her attention back to Larry's companion. Come on, Jasmine! she thought. Turn around. I haven't gone to all this trouble to stare at the back of your head!

Jasmine sat up a little straighter. Now Nancy could see her white hair was short and curly. Nancy's heart pounded wildly. That hair was awfully familiar!

As Jake and Jasmine's TV program switched to a commercial break, Jasmine leaned over to plant a kiss on Jake's cheek, turning her face toward the window. Recognition flooded through Nancy. The woman curled so comfortably next to Jake Sims was none other than Mr. Charles's personal secretary, Elaine Kussack!

15

Den of Thieves

Elaine Kussack! And she hadn't even been on Nancy's suspect list! But now that she knew the truth, Nancy didn't dare stick around a second longer than she had to. It was time to get the police involved as quickly as possible. Ducking below the windowsill, she moved along the porch, motioning Bess and George to follow.

Very quietly, the girls crept over the wooden boards. Nancy hardly dared to breathe. A single noise could spell disaster. Nancy stepped down the porch steps. Three . . . two . . . *creakkk.* The last board gave out a sickening sound.

The girls froze in terror. Had Jake and Jasmine heard them?

They waited without making the slightest move. Only the crickets chirping in the nearby grass broke the night's peace.

Nancy's heart was pounding, but she tried to be optimistic. They were outside, and a thick glass window lay between them and the Simses. She only hoped that it had been enough to muffle the sound.

A minute went by, and still the front door hadn't opened. Maybe they'd finally gotten lucky. Nancy hopped lightly down to the front lawn. Keeping low, she ran across the grass to the paved street beyond.

"I don't get it!" George whispered once they were all away from the house. "If Elaine is Jasmine, how can she and Larry—I mean Jake—get into the vault? She doesn't know the codes to turn off the alarm or anything."

Nancy considered George's point. That was exactly what had kept her from considering Elaine for her suspect list. But now that she thought about it, she could see her mistake.

"You're right," Nancy said. "But you know what? Elaine was in a perfect position to learn all the vital information she needed. Sitting in that office right next to Mr. Charles, she could have spent the whole day spying on him, learning the bank's secrets, memorizing secret codes and combinations."

"You mean, it was Elaine who broke into Mr. Charles's office?" Bess asked, incredulous.

"It's the only answer that makes sense," Nancy reasoned. "No one else could have done it so fast."

"She probably stole the safe-deposit box keys," George guessed, "had copies made, and put them back."

"And on top of everything else, they pretended not to be married so they could both get jobs inside the bank," Nancy said, thinking back to what Jill Adler had said about the bank's rule against married couples. Suddenly it all made sense. "In any case, let's not waste any more time talking. We've got to check on one more thing. Let's get a look at that Skyliner."

Trying to keep gravel crunching to a minimum, the girls moved up the lawn alongside the driveway to the garage. They peered through the windows but couldn't make anything out. The glass was too dirty.

Pulling the sleeve of her dress down over her hand, Nancy used the end of it to wipe away years of grime. Maybe Jake and Jasmine wanted it dirty, Nancy decided, so no one could see what was inside.

Eagerly, she pressed her face up to the tiny peephole she'd cleared. The garage was dark and shadowy with only a little moonlight shining through the dirty windows. But the meager light was enough. As Nancy's eyes adjusted to the light, she saw the unmistakable outline of a '57 Skyliner. Grinning, she stepped aside so Bess and George could see too. One by one they took their turn at the peephole.

"You did it, Nan!" Bess whispered excitedly.

George patted Nancy on the arm. "I'm sure glad I'm on your side. A criminal doesn't have a chance against you."

"Don't be so sure." The female voice came from behind them.

Before Nancy could turn around, she felt the cool firmness of a gun barrel pressing into her back.

"Hello, Elaine," Nancy said calmly. "Or should I call you Jasmine? I wish we could stay, but we were just on our way to the police station."

Jasmine laughed. "'Were' is right. The only place you're going now is to the bottom of Bentley Lake!"

16

Death Ride

"Well, hello, Nancy," came Larry's voice from behind. "I never figured on meeting you again. We poured enough gas through that vent to wipe out a dozen nosy detectives."

Nancy's eyes darted first right, then left, trying to catch a glimpse of a light in a neighbor's window. If people were awake next door, maybe they would notice the commotion in the driveway and call the police. Unfortunately, from where Nancy stood the houses looked dark and silent. She started to turn her head, but the gun barrel dug more painfully into her back.

"No, you don't," Elaine said from the other end of the gun. "Now, I want you three to back away from that garage very slowly. And when I tell you to stop, you stop."

Nancy, Bess, and George backed up one step at a time, their feet sliding uncertainly through the gravel. Nancy was proud to see how bravely her friends were acting. Even Bess didn't let the terror show in her face.

But Nancy could tell they had hung all their hopes on her. She'd gotten them into this miserable situation. It was up to her to get them out.

As they continued to back down the driveway, Nancy's mind raced, trying to formulate a plan. They couldn't run. Jasmine might shoot all three of them dead before they got down the driveway.

No, Nancy's only option was to bluff. "Whatever you're planning to do," she said, "it's pointless. The police are on their way right now."

Jasmine laughed. "Do you know how many times I've heard that line? 'The police are on their way right now,'" Jasmine mimicked. "That's what every clerk has said at every bank we've ever robbed. Sorry, kid, you've got to do better than that. Now, stop right where you are."

Instantaneously Nancy, Bess, and George froze. Quickly Jake moved ahead of them to the garage and hefted open the heavy door. Inside, looking just as though it had driven right out of the movie, was the '57 Ford Skyliner, its top down.

Without bothering to open the car door, Larry hopped in and turned on the ignition. Then, getting out again, he took a heavy coil of rope off a hook in the garage.

"Gotta let 'er warm up," Larry said as he approached the girls. "The Ghost Rider's still got her looks, but she's not as spry as she used to be. Maybe a little like my Jasmine," he added, blowing Elaine a kiss. "Hold out your hands, girls. It's time to practice a little knot tying."

With Elaine's gun still trained on them, the girls had no choice but to obey the Simses' every order. Quickly and efficiently, Jake looped and knotted the rope around Nancy's wrists, then Bess's, then George's,

133

tying them together. He left a length of rope hanging loose on either end.

"Now stay put," Jake ordered. Sprinting back to the car, he hopped in and backed the Skyliner out to where they were standing. Then he leaned over the seat to open the back door. "Get in."

Nancy moved into the car first, struggling for balance as she attempted to slide along the seat without the use of her hands. Once they were all in, Larry tied each end of the rope to the outside door handles of the car. He pulled the cord so tight that Nancy's bound hands were jammed over the top of the Skyliner's left door.

Elaine got into the passenger seat and once again snuggled close to Larry. Slowly Larry pulled out of the driveway and turned onto Lakeview Drive. Nancy craned her neck and looked all around, searching for some escape. But she realized the street was true to its name. It had a spectacular view of Bentley Lake, down below.

"Where are you taking us?" Nancy demanded as they headed up the hill.

Elaine laughed and turned around to face them. "I already told you," she said. "We're sending you to the bottom of Bentley Lake."

"Excuse me," Bess said timidly, "but you're going in the wrong direction. Bentley Lake's behind us." Nancy could hear Bess's voice shaking in the dark beside her.

Elaine laughed again, a cold, tinkling laugh that sent shivers up and down Nancy's spine. "There's no fooling you, is there? The reason we're heading to the top of the hill is that what goes up must come down. Get it?"

"I see you're familiar with the laws of gravity," Nancy said coolly.

"Tell me something," Elaine said, leaning over the front. The gun dangled casually from her hand. "How did you find us? We've been followed by the cops for over thirty years, and no one ever managed to track us down before."

"It was the Skyliner," Nancy explained. "The first time I saw it was when you tossed that rock through my window. The second time was in the movie about your crime career. It was the car that helped make the connection."

Elaine scowled. "I told you we should have gotten rid of the stupid car," she muttered to Larry. "But no, you said, 'We gotta keep the Ghost Rider.' Now you see where it's got us?" Elaine turned back to Nancy. "That was our one mistake," she admitted. "But we're going to correct it right now. We're finally sending the Ghost Rider to the bottom of the lake—with you in it."

"Very clever," Nancy said. "Almost as clever as breaking into the vault and mixing up the jewelry. Not the best way to keep a low profile."

"We were in a hurry!" Elaine yelled. "The automatic timer on the vault slams that door shut after only five minutes if you open the vault after business hours. Six months of planning and all we get is five minutes! That's why it took us so many visits to the vault."

"You'll get twenty years when the police catch you," Nancy said.

Elaine let out her icy, tinkling laugh. "You're a cool character," she said to Nancy. "Fearless. You remind me of myself when I was your age."

Nancy resented being compared to a criminal, but she kept her mouth shut. It wouldn't be a good idea to anger Elaine further.

Elaine's tone grew bitter again. "But if it weren't for you, we could have gotten what we wanted—what

135

we'd planned so long to get. After that first break-in we were going to lay low, wait until everything blew over. But when you showed up, we knew we had to act fast."

"How did you know we were on the case?" Nancy asked. She tugged desperately on the rope that held her wrists tightly against the far side of the car door, but Larry's knots held. He definitely knew how to tie them right.

"I listened in on Mr. Charles's office through the intercom," Elaine explained. "It wasn't hard to rig the thing to work as my own personal bugging device. Came in handy, too, when I needed to learn safe combinations and high security information. Especially because Mr. Charles had this habit of muttering out loud when he opened that big wall safe of his." She laughed dryly.

"And I knew you were a detective as soon as I saw your little notepad," Larry added. "Dead giveaway."

Bess shuddered. "Did he have to use that word— dead?" she whispered.

The old car was having trouble getting up the steep hill. Nancy decided to keep Elaine and Larry talking. "There's one more thing I don't understand," Nancy said. "If you were such big bank robbers, how come you didn't take any of the jewelry? That must have been worth a lot of money."

"Too easy to get caught," Elaine said. "Taking David Baker's stuff, on the other hand, was completely risk free. He's still locked up in the Illinois Pen, so he wouldn't even know it was missing until he managed to get himself let out. And even then, what could he do about it? Go to the police and whine that someone had stolen the money he'd ripped off himself?"

"David Baker!" Larry growled. "He deserves every
136

single day he spends rotting in that jail, and more. No-good double-crossing—"

"And whose fault is that?" asked Elaine angrily. "I never trusted him from the beginning. But you said, 'Let him in. He's got honest eyes.' Honest? Ha! Never trust a crook."

Nancy watched from the backseat. Good. Elaine was getting so riled up, she was spilling the whole story. That would come in handy when they got to the police. *If* they got there. Still, Elaine and Larry's argument provided a perfect cover for an escape attempt. If only she had a plan . . . One thing she did know—keeping them talking was good, any way she played it.

"What did Baker do?" Nancy asked, pushing for the conversation to continue. Larry had stopped the car at a cross street, but soon it would near the crest of the hill. The prospect of a return trip down to the lake—without a driver—was looking more and more horrible.

"Well, nothing at first," Elaine told her. "In fact, he was real useful when money was short. Because he was a counterfeiter, he could just print us out a couple of thousand whenever we needed it. But then, the night of our last job, he pulled the biggest double-cross of the century, and got away with all the money. That was our biggest job too. Half a million in cash."

Nancy listened carefully, but at the same time her eyes searched out the Skyliner's every detail. There had to be something helpful—something sharp—that could cut these ropes. Nancy's gaze slid over the car's gleaming metal.

And then she saw it. At the point where the retractable hood slid into the body of the car, a small jagged piece stood out, part of the hood's mechanism. Maybe, just maybe, it would be sharp enough to slice through the ropes. If only she could reach it. Nancy eased her hands over, hoping that Elaine wouldn't notice. But the rope pulled taut too early, holding her hands just two inches from her goal.

Nancy felt like screaming. Their only chance, and she couldn't reach it! Still, even in the agony of frustration, Nancy realized she had to keep the conversation going. It was her only way of distracting the Simses. "Why . . . why was that your last job?" she fumbled.

"Somebody ratted on us," Elaine said bitterly. "Someone in the gang. We never found out who, but he must have let the police know, because they were waiting for us. When we stepped out of the bank, we were completely surrounded."

"The odds were incredible—like five cops to each one of us," Larry added.

"The rest of the gang was caught," Elaine said. "Boy, I was more than mad. But we managed to get to the main road and hitch a ride on the back of a laundry truck. Too bad for us Baker was carrying all the cash. He got away too."

" 'Mad' just doesn't describe how furious we were," Larry agreed.

"We were going to hunt him down," Elaine confessed, "but we'd already saved up so much money, we figured it was a good time to retire. So we changed our names and moved around a lot, just to keep the police off our tail."

"What happened to Baker?" Nancy asked. She pulled hard on the rope, tugging it toward the jagged metal that was their only hope. Her hands slid over about a quarter of an inch. That still left one and three quarters to go. She was totally frustrated. The rope simply wasn't long enough to reach the metal piece.

"I suppose he did the same," Elaine said. "Only he wasn't as lucky as we were. This one detective just wouldn't give up. The guy finally tracked him down right here in Bentley. We heard about it when he was arrested, and we celebrated."

"For many years we thought Baker was out of our lives for good," Larry said. "But then, about a year ago, we ran into a counterfeit printer who'd been cellmates with Baker in the Illinois Pen. He told us Baker was storing his counterfeit plates in a safe-deposit box in the bank here. He was planning to start printing again as soon as he got out."

"The plates!" Nancy exclaimed. Deeper down, though, her fear was mounting as she saw the top of the hill drawing near fast. They were almost there, and she still didn't have a plan. "So that's what you were looking for, not the half a million dollars! But why did you need them if you had all that money?"

"Hey, thirty years is a long time," Elaine informed her. "We've lived pretty well on our bank money for all that time, but now we're running out. The way we figured it, those plates were all we needed to get us by for the rest of our lives. Whenever we needed it, we'd just make some fresh money. Besides, it would be a great way to get our revenge on David."

"Here we are," Larry said as they reached the top of the hill. "Are you ready for your return trip?" He sounded almost friendly as he said it, as if the trip wouldn't mean the end for Nancy and her friends. Larry spun the car into a U-turn, then switched off the ignition. "Here's where we get out," he said to Elaine.

Nancy looked around. There had to be someone or

something nearby that could stop the terrible finale that Larry and Elaine had planned for them.

"Please wait!" Nancy cried, desperate to buy time. "You can't leave before you tell me the end of the story."

"Yes," said George, guessing what Nancy was trying to do. "At least tell us how you got into the vault."

"And how two bank robbers got jobs working inside a bank," Bess added.

Elaine laughed. "I guess it can't hurt. The only ones you'll be able to spill to are the fish." She addressed Bess's question first. "Forgery is one of the simplest crimes there is," she explained, sounding almost like a schoolteacher as she spoke. "We made ourselves some phony documents and résumés so we could pass a security check. It was a cinch." She snapped her fingers.

"And you needed those jobs in the bank so you could learn the security system, right?" Nancy guessed. Her mind was racing. She just had to think of a way out!

"Right," Elaine confirmed.

"Security's a lot trickier now than it was in the good years before we retired," added Larry. "At first, it was hard with all those electronic gizmos and such. We didn't grow up with computers, like you youngsters. But"—he smiled proudly—"we learned it."

Elaine picked up the story where her husband had left off. "Jake knew the vault combination, and I learned the alarm code and the combination to Mr. Charles's safe by spying on him. That's how we got the keys to the boxes. Actually, I wanted to get those keys, copy them, and return them to the safe before Mr. Charles noticed they were gone. But that afternoon he happened to need something in the safe, and he discovered they were missing."

"A piece of bad luck, that was," Larry commented. "It meant we had to open Mr. Charles's safe a second time, trash his office to make it look like a robbery, and then return the keys."

"It did give us the chance to leave Evelyn Sobel's glove, though, to throw you off the track."

"How'd you slip past the security guard upstairs?" Nancy asked.

"We never left the bank after work," Elaine replied. "We just slipped downstairs when the guard was on the other side of the building. We still wore masks, though, just in case the guard saw us. He never did, though."

"Let me tell you, there are hundreds of hiding places in that bank," Larry continued. "Don, the janitor, knew every one of them."

"Don!" Nancy exclaimed. "Was he in on this too?" She just couldn't imagine the mild-mannered man fitting in with these two hardened criminals. In fact, it seemed almost comical that she'd ever entertained the thought that he could be Jake Sims, married to Evelyn Sobel as Jasmine.

Larry let out a guffaw. "Don, a bank robber? No way! That guy's a patsy, a total innocent. All I had to do was pal around with him when he came down to mop up the vault, and he'd spill tons of valuable information. And he didn't even realize he was doing it!"

"But didn't the night guard hear you when you opened the vault?" Nancy wanted to know.

"We waited till late, when we knew he was asleep," Elaine said.

"He always falls asleep," Larry put in. "He told me so himself once."

"Then we chloroformed him," Elaine said. "To make sure he wouldn't wake up too soon."

141

"So you broke in and started to open the boxes," Nancy concluded. "But you had just five minutes before the door would start to close automatically."

"Right again," Elaine said. "You know, you're smart." She looked at Nancy with admiration. "We could have used someone like you back in the old days. Too bad you're going to be very dead in just a few minutes. Jake, perhaps it's time for us to say bon voyage?"

Nancy felt cold dread grip her heart. Larry just couldn't start that car before she came up with a plan! "Wait!" she cried out. "I've got just a few more questions. Please, I'm dying of curiosity." She gulped as she realized her unfortunate choice of words.

Elaine and Larry laughed. "Go ahead," Larry said to his wife. "We may be bank robbers, even murderers, but we're not completely heartless."

"How . . . how did you get out of the bank?" Nancy fumbled, searching for every tiny detail that hadn't been explained. "Even if the security guard was asleep, you still would have had to pass the TV cameras."

"We never left," Elaine told her. "We hid out in the bank all night until it opened in the morning."

"And the grenade," George said. "I kept wondering why the thieves didn't use a real one, but of course you couldn't with Larry down there."

Larry nodded. "That was meant only to scare you. After all, we wouldn't want to damage the vault. I'm glad we prepared ourselves well, though, with the grenades and the poison gas," he added. "We'd kept those stashed away in case anything went wrong— which it did, just as soon as you three showed up."

"You two are just full of tricks," Bess commented

grimly. "Like when one of you almost ran Nancy down on Mountain Avenue."

"That was me," Elaine said. "I was on my lunch break."

Elaine sighed, patting Nancy's hand in an almost motherly fashion. "You know, it really is going to be a shame to get rid of someone with your brains." Then she frowned. "But because of those brains of yours, Jake and I are going to have to move on without the counterfeiting plates. This bank's gotten too hot to handle." She turned to her husband. "And now, it really is time, Jake."

Nancy's heart pumped pure adrenaline. Could this really be it? Were she, George, and Bess going to end it all here, in a '57 Skyliner at the bottom of Bentley Lake?

Getting out of the car, Elaine gazed down at the lake. "Looks awfully pretty, doesn't it?" she asked.

Although Nancy didn't want to, she found herself looking down the steep incline of the quiet road and into the murky water.

"I hate long goodbyes," Elaine said. With a short wave of her hand, she turned and walked away from the car.

Now Larry opened the car door and swung one leg out. "Goodbye, Ghost Rider," he said, patting the white metal. "I'll miss you." Then he turned his attention to the girls. "This is one roller-coaster ride you'll remember for the rest of your lives," he said. "Which won't exactly be a long time." Laughing, he shifted the car into neutral, took his foot off the brake, and hopped out. Instantly the car started to roll down the hill.

The convertible quickly picked up speed. The wind

off the lake whipped harshly in the girls' faces as they raced downward, faster and faster, hurtling ever closer toward their watery grave.

Think! Nancy ordered her brain. *Think!* But there was no way out. And the lake was only seconds below them.

17

Foiled!

As the car made its death dash toward the lake, Bess
screamed, but her voice was swallowed up in the
rushing of the wind. Nancy knew she had to get her
friends—and herself—out of this. Somehow she had
to reach the jagged metal piece at the back of the car,
cut her bonds, and stop the car!

"Lean to your left!" Nancy yelled to Bess and
George.

"What?" Bess screamed back.

"Left! Left!" Nancy shouted, leaning hard.

Although she was tied to the right side of the car,
George threw her body sideways, shoving Bess with
her. The girls shifted on the leather seats just slightly.
It wasn't much, but it was just enough. In one swift
movement Nancy hooked her hands under the jagged
metal. Frantically, she rubbed the rope against it at
record speed. Bentley Lake was approaching even
faster.

Twwang. Nancy felt a snap, and the rope unraveled

away from her hands. With only seconds left she leapt over the front seat and practically fell behind the steering wheel. Using every ounce of strength she had left, she slammed both feet on the brake pedal. Behind her she heard Bess and George scream as the car screeched and skidded off the road. It hit two garbage cans, wrecked a good stretch of lawn, and jerked to a halt just inches from the shoreline.

Bess and George lurched forward in their seats, then whipped backward again, still held by the rope.

Nancy let out a whoosh of pent-up breath. Then she turned to face her friends. "You guys okay?" she asked as she quickly began working at untying Bess and George.

"I hate to say it," said George, "but it's a good thing we were tied to the car. Otherwise we would have been thrown right into the lake. I think we're both fine, though."

"I can't believe it!" Bess cried. "Nancy, you're a hero!" She shook the ropes from her wrists, then leapt over the seat to give Nancy a huge, grateful hug.

Reassured that her friends were safe, Nancy shifted the car into reverse, backed a few yards up the hill, then turned the vehicle around.

"Where are we going?" Bess asked. "Don't you think we've had enough thrills for one day?"

"Bess, we can still stop Larry and Elaine—Jake and Jasmine—but we have to do it right away," Nancy explained. "They're not going to take their time getting out of Bentley. We have to be faster than they are."

As Nancy started up Lakeview Drive, she spotted a flashing red-and-blue light far up the hill. A police car! If only she could flag it down, they could radio the state police to put out a bulletin on Jake and Jasmine.

Nancy slid the stick shift into a higher gear. Instead

146

of speeding up, however, the car suddenly choked, sputtered, and stalled. Giving the key another turn, Nancy pressed her foot on the accelerator, but the car wouldn't respond.

"Wouldn't you know it? After thirty years, this car gives out on us just when we need it most. Come on. We'll have to go the rest of the way on foot." Like Larry before them, they hopped out of the car without opening the doors, then hotfooted it up the hill.

"*Stop right where you are!*" A loud female voice cut through the night, her words amplified by a bullhorn.

Startled, Nancy, Bess, and George jumped out of the way as a second police car skidded to a halt right at their feet, its lights still flashing.

"*Now step away from the car with your hands up,*" the officer with the bullhorn directed.

With a sinking heart, Nancy realized who that tough female voice belonged to. Captain Elizabeth Steiner. Matters looked even worse when a short, stocky policeman approached them, gun drawn. Sergeant Ramirez had finally caught up with them. His once-friendly face was now scowling.

"Thought you could put a few over on me, huh?" he asked. "First the 'school project' and then the phony phone call. You made me look like a fool in front of my boss. With all the lies you've told, how can you expect us to believe you when you say you aren't the bank robbers, you just happened to be at the scene of the crime?"

"But we're not the crooks!" Nancy cried. "And now we know who they really are. It's—"

"I'm not interested in any more of your tricks or lies," Ramirez said, cutting Nancy off. "If you have anything else to say, wait until your lawyer gets here."

Captain Steiner emerged from the police car dangling three pairs of handcuffs. "That was a mighty quick recovery you all made," she said. "A few hours ago you weren't well enough to answer questions. Now we find you speeding around Bentley in a Skyliner in the middle of the night. Not trying to make a getaway by any chance?"

"No!" Nancy cried. "But Jake and Jasmine Sims will be if you don't go after them right away."

"I don't know any people called Sims," Captain Steiner said. "And I'm certainly not going to dash off after them—assuming they exist at all—before I've got you and your friends locked securely in jail!" She raised the first pair of handcuffs. "Ms. Drew, would you like to be first?"

But before Captain Steiner could snap the handcuffs on, a second police siren split the night and a department car sped up, flashing its blue-and-red light. The car screeched to a halt in front of the small group. In another instant Nancy recognized her father's car following on the first vehicle's bumper.

"Wait!" Nancy's father cried as he and Mr. Charles jumped out of his car.

"Dad!" Nancy cried.

Carson Drew stepped between his daughter and Captain Steiner. "You are in serious trouble, Nancy," he said.

"No kidding," Nancy answered.

Now Carson turned to the police officer. "Captain," he said, "you've made a mistake."

"Oh no." Captain Steiner waved away the explanation. "We're not falling for that again."

"Let me explain," Nancy's father began. "Earlier this evening, Mr. Charles and I returned to the hospital. At the same time, your officers were in the midst of discovering that the girls were missing. We heard you'd

148

issued an all-points bulletin on them." Nancy's father wet his lips. She'd seen him do it a million times in court, when he was trying hard to convince a jury.

"I was in the girls' room while the police searched it, and I noticed Nancy's notebook lying on her bed. It was open to an address." Carson produced the notebook from his pocket and showed it to Captain Steiner. "Two twenty-two Lakeview Drive. Knowing my daughter as well as I do, I realized that was where she'd probably gone. I persuaded one of your men to accompany me there."

Carson Drew started toward the second police car. "Will you follow me, please?"

Eyeing him suspiciously, and with one hand firmly on Nancy's arm, Captain Steiner headed after Carson Drew.

Nancy's father paused before the back door of the police car. "Just a block away from 222 Lakeview Drive," he continued, "I found two people attempting to hot-wire my daughter's car."

Carson threw open the door with a flourish. There was a collective gasp as everyone recognized the couple inside. It was Larry Jaye and Elaine Kussack— better known as Jake and Jasmine Sims.

"They might have been a little before your time," Nancy told the police captain, "but they're two of the most wanted bank robbers in America."

"It's true," the police officer in the car affirmed to Captain Steiner. "I radioed for Boggs to look it up in the computer back at the station. The whole story's true!"

"And you were just doing your jobs," Nancy replied understandingly.

Captain Steiner shook her hand apologetically. "You know, now that you're done working at the bank, we could really use your help on our police force. I don't suppose you'd be interested in coming to work for us? All three of you? You'd be on a very fast track."

Nancy laughed. "Thanks, but I think we've gone fast enough for one night!"

"Okay, you two, start talking," Mr. Charles said. He leaned back in his plush office armchair, glancing from Ms. Sobel to Maurice and back again. The two employees were hunched over, looking unhappy. Mr. Charles's tone was stern, but there was a twinkle in his eye. "You first, Evelyn."

Nancy folded one knee over the other and leaned forward, eager to hear Ms. Sobel's explanation. She may have solved the big mystery, but she still didn't have a clue about the assistant bank manager's late hours and frequent trips to the vault. She could tell that Bess and George, sitting beside her, were just dying to know the reasons too.

Ms. Sobel looked down at her hands, studying her fingernails. "It's foolish," she told her boss. "You'll think it's unprofessional."

"No matter what it is," Mr. Charles pressed, "it can't be as bad as what we suspected you of."

Ms. Sobel cleared her throat. "I was writing a . . ." She coughed, embarrassed, covering over the last word so nobody could understand her.

"A what?" Mr. Charles asked.

"A—a novel," Ms. Sobel said in a low voice.

"A novel!" Mr. Charles roared.

Ms. Sobel nodded, looking up at him fearfully. "Well, why didn't you just say so?" Mr. Charles laughed. "You didn't have to go around hiding it like it was a crime."

"I didn't want anybody to know," Ms. Sobel ex-

150

plained. "I wasn't sure if it was any good. I figured if I ever sold it, then I could tell people."

"So that's what you were working on with the computer that night," Nancy guessed.

Ms. Sobel nodded. "I don't have a word processor at home, so I used the one in the office. And I didn't want to store it in the computer's memory because then any employee in the bank could get into it, so I stored it on a disk and kept it locked up in the vault."

"That explains why you made so many trips downstairs," Nancy commented.

"What's the book about?" George asked the assistant bank manager.

Ms. Sobel smiled. "It's about a woman who works in a bank—where nothing exciting ever happens!"

At first there was a stunned silence. Then, one by one, the group began to giggle. The giggles erupted into laughter, the laughter into a roar.

"A bank where nothing ever happens!" Bess exclaimed. "No wonder you felt weird about telling people. Around here, no one would believe such a place existed!"

Now Ms. Sobel turned to face the girls. "I—I really want to apologize," she said softly. "I wasn't very nice to any of you."

"I'll say," Bess piped up, and Nancy nudged her to be quiet.

"I guess I was just feeling threatened," she said, "when I saw Mr. Charles hiring people without even speaking to me. I even worried that he might be getting ready to fire me."

Mr. Charles shook his head. "Of course not! And actually, I guess I owe you an apology too. I was so busy being nervous about the vault that I didn't think about how you'd feel. I'm sorry."

"Apologies accepted all around," Nancy said.

Mr. Charles turned his attention to Maurice. "I can't wait to hear what *you've* got to say," he commented. "All that expensive jewelry you gave Jill! I can't imagine where you got it from."

Maurice shook his head. "I'm sure I'll sound just as foolish," he told them. "It's true that the jewelry didn't cost me a cent. But I didn't steal it either."

"Where did you get it, then?" Bess asked.

"I inherited a few pieces from my grandmother," Maurice said. "The diamond ring, the bracelet, and a ruby necklace. I was her only grandchild, so I got everything she had."

"Boy," Bess said, "the way you were talking, it sounded like you were a millionaire!"

"I guess that's how I wanted it to sound," Maurice said sheepishly. "I was trying to impress Jill. Especially after that ridiculous scene I made when I broke it off with her."

"You didn't have to do that," Nancy chided. "Jill really loves you. She was devastated when you told her there was another girl."

Maurice hung his head, looking one hundred percent ashamed. "That other girl never existed," he admitted. "I made her up so that Jill wouldn't find out I'd lied about the money. But then I realized I couldn't live without her."

"I think Jill knows that now," Nancy said, smiling. "But I think it's going to take a while before she can trust you again. You hurt her very badly."

"I know," Maurice agreed, his voice low. "I just hope I can make it up to her."

"Well," Nancy said, uncrossing her legs and getting up to go. "I can't say it's been easy, but my internship at the Bentley Bank certainly has been action-packed."

Bess swung the strap of her purse over her shoulder, and George stood up, smoothing the front of her blouse.

"Thanks again, all of you," Mr. Charles said, rising. "I wish you'd accept a reward. At least something small to show you my appreciation."

Nancy shook her head. "I was just glad to help."

"Well, I'll tell you what," Mr. Charles said. "How about a free checking account for each of you? I'll hold them open in your name until you need to use them."

"Okay," Nancy said. "Thanks."

Mr. Charles opened the door to a large closet and disappeared inside. A moment later he reemerged with three cardboard boxes. "Here," he said, handing one to each of the girls."

"What are those?" George asked.

"Toaster ovens," Mr. Charles replied. "It's the free gift you get when you open a checking account at Bentley Bank!"

Nancy laughed, feeling touched.

The girls had only one more stop in Bentley before heading home, and that was Bentley General Hospital. When they'd sneaked out, they'd left a few belongings behind, including the now long-overdue copy of *Jake and Jasmine.*

"I guess we should return this before we leave town," Bess said, tossing the cartridge over to Nancy after they had retrieved it.

"No way," Nancy said. She tucked the cassette under her arm. "I still want to find out how the film ends."

Half an hour later Nancy, Bess, and George were comfortably sprawled on the couch in Nancy's den, a bowl of popcorn on the coffee table in front of them.

Nancy loaded the video into the VCR, and the film picked up in the tattoo parlor. From there to the end of the tape it was just one bank robbery after another, and on to the big finale when the two love-bird robbers hopped a laundry truck out of the police trap.

"Gee," Bess said through a mouthful of popcorn. "It's a lot less scary on film than it was in real life."

"You realize they'll have to do a sequel now," George added. *Jake and Jasmine Two.* Starring Bess Marvin, George Fayne, and Nancy Drew!"